The girl turr[...]
frowned. "You [...]
she said. "You [...] ...ave right away."

"We've rented the flat above the shop,"
said Pip. "We're living here now."

"Well, you've made a massive mistake.
Get out of here. Seriously."

"I don't understand…" started Pip.

"Look," the girl said. "I'll spell it out."
She adopted a slow, exaggerated tone.
"If you stay here, something
extremely bad is going
to happen!"

To Freddie, Rupert and Toby

First published in the UK in 2023 by Usborne Publishing Limited, Usborne House, 83-85 Saffron Hill, London EC1N 8RT, England. usborne.com

Usborne Verlag, Usborne Publishing Limited, Prüfeninger Str. 20, 93049 Regensburg, Deutschland VK Nr. 17560

Text © Cat Gray, 2023

Cover illustrations by David Dean © Usborne Publishing, 2023

A CIP catalogue record for this book is available from the British Library.

ISBN 9781801310048   JFMAMJJ SOND/23   7518/1

Printed and bound using 100% renewable energy at CPI Group (UK) Ltd, Croydon, CR0 4YY.

THE SPIRIT SNATCHER

CAT GRAY

USBORNE

1

On the Move

All parents are challenging on some level, but Pip Ruskin's parents were off the scale. Their unrelenting weirdness had blighted the first twelve years of his life and it seemed as if things were about to get even worse.

"It's a dream come true," sighed Mrs Ruskin, as she stretched out in the front seat of their battered turquoise car, a large jar of home-made pickles in her lap.

"No, it isn't," corrected Pip. He was squashed in the back seat, along with a dozen bulging suitcases. "I don't want to live in London."

"When I was your age, I'd have given anything to live in the middle of a city like this," said his father, grinning at him madly in the rear-view mirror. He was so excited, he looked as if he was about to explode. "Isn't it wonderful?"

Pip stared miserably out at the never-ending traffic jam. Massive grey buildings reared up on either side of the wide road, and people hurried through the rain, their hoods up or hiding behind umbrellas. For the millionth time that day, Pip wished they hadn't had to move.

It wasn't that Pip liked their old life in Norwich. It was more that he had learned how to deal with it. Living with Mr and Mrs Ruskin was not exactly easy, and Pip had become an expert at damage limitation.

There were the obvious things that made them different from other people's parents, like his mother's hair, which was silvery grey and so long that she could sit on it, and her round little glasses that made her look like an owl. There was his father's yellow corduroy suit, which he wore every single day and was so bright he had once been mistaken for a clown. Some things were less noticeable at first, but still not great, like his father's habit of singing to himself or his mother's extreme forgetfulness, or the way that his parents held hands and kissed in public – not the peck-on-the-cheek kind of kiss, but the slobbery sort that goes on for too long and makes other people stare. Individually, none of these things were too bad, but when you put them all together it became a problem. The more his parents stood out, the harder it was for Pip to fit in. In fact, fitting in, or at the very least, not having anyone notice him, was Pip's main ambition in life.

"How about a fermented Brussels sprout, darling?" said Mrs Ruskin. She flipped open the glass lid of the pickle jar and instantly a hideous smell, like rotten vinegary eggs, filled the car. She twisted round, waving the jar under Pip's nose. He choked, trying not to be sick, and opened the window. He stuck his head out and breathed in the petrol fumes gratefully.

"Don't you want one?" asked his mother, still holding out the reeking jar.

"I'm not hungry," said Pip, then felt bad when he saw her face fall.

"But I'd love one anyway," he amended. He prised a slimy green Brussels sprout out of the jar as his stomach lurched again and the bile rose in his throat.

Mrs Ruskin beamed at him. She was a great believer in gut-friendly food. All their meals involved large quantities of every sort of fermented vegetable you can imagine. Even worse, she insisted on making Pip a packed lunch every day. After five long hours of sweating away in Pip's schoolbag, Mrs Ruskin's carefully prepared lunchbox of mackerel, broccoli and home-made pickles inevitably transformed into a hand grenade of appalling smelliness. Pip dreaded opening the lid. It was like setting off a stink bomb – the ripe bin-lorry stench would hit him full in the face then whoosh outwards, spreading across the room and causing everybody to do a stadium wave of nose-wrinkling, face-scrunching and gagging noises. After the first few times, Pip learned that it was better if he ate his lunch alone, in the furthest corner of the schoolyard. With lunches like his, it had been impossible to make any friends. But his mother looked so surprised and upset whenever he mentioned he didn't like her food that he had long since dropped the subject.

He tossed the Brussels sprout out of the car window when no one was looking, and wondered what his new school would be like. At least he didn't have to start until after the half-term break at Halloween, so he had several weeks of freedom before he had to figure out how to blend in all over again. He was pretty certain that his parents would be as peculiar in London as they had been in Norwich.

In the next lane, a Range Rover had pulled up beside them. A boy a few years older than Pip was sitting in the passenger seat, shaking with laughter. He had his phone pressed to the window and seemed to be videoing the

Ruskins' car. For a moment, Pip stared at him, wondering what was so funny. The fact that the little car was twenty years old? The bright turquoise paint? A second later, Pip realized what it was and his heart sank. The chaos of the move and leaving in the early-morning darkness had made him forget his usual routine. He had forgotten to clean the car.

"Dad?" he croaked. There was no reply. Mr Ruskin was singing to himself again.

"Dad!" he tried again. He kicked the back of the driver's seat and the singing stopped.

"What is it, son?"

"The car," said Pip. "Did you remember to clean it?"

"Of course not," replied his father. "I don't know why you're always so worried about it. Who cares about a little mess?"

To describe what had happened to the outside of the car as "a little mess" was like calling the prime minister " a little famous" or the devil "a little evil".

Pip didn't need to see the video the boy in the next lane was clearly uploading to the internet to know what the outside of the car looked like. He knew that the roof, the bonnet and all four sides of it were covered in a thick layer of lumpy bird poo.

9

The problem had started four years ago, when a pair of swallows decided to build their nest in the garage, which also doubled as a storage space for Mr Ruskin's unsuccessful antiques business. There was only one area that wasn't crammed to the rafters with old furniture, and that happened to be the spot right above the car. Soon, the swallows multiplied, more nests appeared, and every single bird decided that the Ford Fiesta was their preferred toilet spot.

"Swallows nesting in your building are lucky," Mr Ruskin had said. "And if a bird poos on you, that's lucky too. So if we have swallows living in our garage *and* pooing on our car, why that means we'll have more luck than we'll know what to do with."

It had not been very lucky for Pip.

Every afternoon during the summer term, his father would drive up to Pip's school far too early and park right in front of the gates, in full view of Pip's classroom. Before long, someone would spot it, a note would be passed around, and by the time the final bell rang, the entire class would be collapsing with laughter and Pip would be bright red with embarrassment. He'd rush out of school as fast as possible, hoping that if he was quick enough, he might be able to get away before any more students got a chance to see it. But it was no use. He had become firmly associated with the Poo-mobile, as it was known, and although everyone usually forgot about it by winter, the swallows would return the following spring and the whole horrible cycle would begin again. This year, the swallows had stayed unusually late. They were obviously enjoying themselves.

Since he was ten, Pip had covered the car with a sheet of plastic each evening, and every morning he carefully cleaned off all the bird poo that had missed the sheet. But last night he hadn't remembered to put on the plastic sheet, and they had left so early in the morning that it had still been dark. He hadn't even thought about what might have happened to the car during the night.

The traffic lights turned green and they lurched forwards. The pile of suitcases toppled over and crashed on top of Pip. By the time he'd freed himself they were heading through a maze of city streets.

"Nearly there," said Mr Ruskin, squinting at the satnav. They went past a large auction house, its windows plastered with images of treasures they'd sold, past galleries displaying gold-framed paintings and strangely shaped sculptures, and office buildings with revolving glass doors. It was not the sort of place where families usually lived, but Mrs Ruskin was a scientist and had got a new job in London, which meant they all had to move home just six weeks into the new school year. Pip's father had come across an advert for a shop to rent in one of London's most famous antiques districts, which had a flat above it. The rent was very cheap, and as it had always been Mr Ruskin's ambition to open an antiques shop, they'd taken on the lease without even having seen the place and promptly booked a removal van.

"We're here!" announced Mr Ruskin. He looked round expectantly, then frowned. "At least, it says we're here."

"We can't be," replied Mrs Ruskin. "The shop's in Elbow Alley and we're still on Magwitch Street."

Leaving his parents puzzling over the satnav, Pip opened the car door and climbed out, rubbing his arm from where the suitcases had bruised him. He took a few steps away from the car, so no one would think that he had anything to do with it, but then he realized there was no one around anyway. It was a Sunday and the street was completely deserted. The offices were closed and so was the auction house, their windows dark. The only place that was lit up was a grand-looking gallery, where two huge old portraits stood in the windows, illuminated against a blood-red background. One of the paintings was of a stern, sallow man in a ruff, the other of a woman who looked remarkably like a poodle.

Pip pushed at the gallery door, intending to ask for directions, but it didn't open. There was a bell, but something stopped him from pressing the button. Perhaps it was the unfriendly expressions on the pair of portraits, but the place felt intimidating. As he backed away, he spotted something. An archway was sandwiched between the side of the gallery and the office building on the other side, so narrow and tucked away that you'd hardly notice it was there.

Beyond the tunnel of the arch, there was a narrow little street, lined with shops. It looked like it belonged to a different time. The buildings were high and teetering, looming towards each other. Billows of steam from an air vent swirled about like mist. A painted pub sign swung creakily in the autumn breeze. Pip spotted a street sign fixed a little way down the dark passage. It was Elbow Alley. He stared for a moment in surprise, unable to believe that this peculiar place was his new home.

His parents had got out of the car now and were gazing around Magwitch Street in their usual way – his mother looked distracted and dreamy, as if her mind was on other things, while his father was bouncing up and down on the soles of his feet, as if he couldn't contain his excitement.

"It's down here!" called Pip. He was too intrigued to wait for them, so he went on ahead, through the archway and into the shadowy alley.

2

An Unwelcome Beginning

The further Pip went down Elbow Alley, the stranger it got. A rat scuttled out, and when it saw Pip it sat up on its hind legs and stared at him instead of running away. The shops weren't like normal shops. The doors were shut, and most of them seemed to be doing their best to make sure that no one would be tempted to go in. A shop called The Pickled Trout had a giant mouldy cheese displayed in the window, while the one next to it was crammed with an extraordinary quantity of junk.

"Wow," said a familiar voice.

Pip whirled around and saw his parents. They were both carrying a suitcase in each hand and their eyes were shining brightly. His father was gazing into the junk-filled windows of Dribs & Drabs with the expression of someone whose wildest dreams have just come true.

His mother was humming a folk tune.

"Which shop's ours?" asked Pip.

"It's number thirty-two, I think," said Mrs Ruskin. One of the suitcases slipped from her hand and it fell open, scattering her clothes all over the ground.

"Oh dear," she said, vaguely, setting down the other case.

Pip scrambled about, retrieving his mother's collection of sensible trousers, white lab coats and pickle jars. He stuffed them back into her case and forced the clasps shut again.

"I can carry it," he said, and hefted it up.

"Thank you, darling," she said. She smiled at him, then started to hum again.

Pip had always felt an inexplicable need to protect his parents. They seemed unusually helpless when it came to navigating daily life, and their eccentric behaviour somehow made them appear even more vulnerable. Pip often had the sensation that he had to look after them, even though he knew it should be the other way around.

He continued up the alley, scanning each doorway for numbers while his parents lagged behind, pausing to exclaim over the hat shop or admire the display in the bookshop window.

As he approached the pub, he stopped dead.

A girl was standing in the dark doorway of The Ragged Hare, her arms folded, watching him. A small wiry-haired dog stood next to her, so still that it took Pip a moment to realize it was a living animal. The girl was about Pip's age, with brown skin, a mass of springy curls, and a flamboyant taste in clothes. She was wearing a gold jumpsuit and a denim jacket that was embroidered all over with brightly coloured flowers. Pip caught her eye, and she stared back at him suspiciously.

"What?" she said, curtly.

"Do you know where number thirty-two is?" he asked. For a moment, Pip thought the girl wasn't going to answer, but eventually she unfolded her arms.

"Next door," she said, pointing and still looking at him with a curious expression, as if he was from a different planet. "Why?"

"We're moving in," said Pip, nodding down the alley to where his parents were still peering through the bookshop window.

The girl turned to look at them, then frowned. "You shouldn't have come here," she said. "You need to leave right away."

"We've rented the flat above the shop," said Pip. "We're living here now."

"Well, you've made a massive mistake. Get out of here. Seriously."

"I don't understand…" started Pip, beginning to feel confused at the girl's strange reaction.

"You lot are outsiders," she said, impatiently. "I can see that a mile off."

"What do you mean, 'outsiders'? And why do you care if we live here or not?" asked Pip.

For a moment, the girl looked worried, as if she'd said too much. Her dog gave a low growl.

"None of your business," she said eventually, her voice distinctly cold now.

"Well, it's too late – we're living here. There's nothing you can do about it."

"Look," the girl said, sounding exasperated. "I'll spell it out."

She adopted a slow, exaggerated tone, the sort you use when you're speaking to someone behind a thick pane of glass.

"IF YOU STAY HERE, SOMETHING EXTREMELY BAD IS GOING TO HAPPEN!"

Pip wasn't quite sure if it was meant as a warning or as a threat.

"Who's that you're speaking to, Pip?" called his father.

"Is it one of our new neighbours?"

But the girl had already disappeared back inside The Ragged Hare, without saying another word. Pip peered into the shadowy pub but there was no sign of her or the dog.

Her words still rang in his ears. So far, London was turning out to be even worse than Norwich. Pip felt like crying, like going back and sitting in the car until his parents agreed to drive him somewhere else. But his mother and father were looking so pleased and excited that he knew there was no chance of that.

"Our place is just here," said Pip in a heavy voice, and pointed at the peeling brown door. The house had a curved shop window that had been covered over with old newspapers. Mr Ruskin pulled a key out of his pocket and struggled to turn it in the rusty lock.

"There we go!" he cried at last, as the lock gave way and the front door groaned as it juddered open.

Inside was disgusting. The shop on the ground floor was covered in dust. Their living accommodation was up a steep flight of stairs, which was covered with mouldy brown carpet. The previous tenants must have used these rooms as an office, because ancient computers with tangled cables were stacked up in a corner of the sitting room along with piles of cardboard folders and an old television.

The kitchen was tiny, with iron bars across the single small window. The countertops were a greyish plastic, while the tiles above them were a reddish brown. A semi-melted microwave stood in one corner while a used fire blanket was clipped to the wall above it – someone had tried to stuff it back into its container, even though it was covered in scorch marks.

"Let's just leave," suggested Pip, who was still pondering over what the strange girl had said to him. "We can't stay here."

"Don't be silly, Pip," said Mrs Ruskin, but she was beginning to appear uncomfortable.

There was the sound of cheerful singing and Mr Ruskin bounced into the kitchen.

"Don't look so glum!" he cried, flinging his arms wide. "Once we've moved all our things in, it'll be just like our old house."

"I'm sure you're right," agreed Mrs Ruskin. "I wonder where the bathroom is?"

She wandered back into the hall. They heard her open another door, scream, then slam it shut again. When she came back into the kitchen, Pip recognized the expression on her face. It was the look she always got when things got too much. He knew what was coming next.

"I'm going to pop over to the laboratory," she said, glancing at her watch. "Just to let them know I've arrived. I know it's a weekend, but some members of the team will still be there."

"We'll have things shipshape for when you get back," said Mr Ruskin. He was the only one who still seemed to be in good spirits. Mrs Ruskin practically fled from the house, towards the comfort of her new workplace. That was the strange thing about his mother. At home, she was incredibly absent-minded, but when it came to her job, she was very focused.

"The removal van won't be here until four," said Mr Ruskin, who was rummaging in one of his suitcases. He pulled out a kettle and a squashed box of teabags. "We might as well make ourselves at home."

Despite the tea, the flat didn't feel any more comfortable as the afternoon went on. The removal men didn't show up until five o'clock, and they weren't too happy when they found out that they couldn't drive their lorry down the alley, but had to park on the main road instead. Pip and his father had to help them carry box after box, passing them from one to the other in a human chain. It seemed to go on for ever because of the enormous amount of junk that Mr Ruskin had collected over the years.

"There's at least three times the normal amount of furniture here," said the driver, staring into the back of the van with his forehead wrinkled. "You sure it's all yours?"

"It's for my antiques business," said Mr Ruskin proudly, and passed a three-legged chair to Pip, who added it to the growing pile on the shop floor.

Pip had a feeling they were being watched – he saw a curtain twitch from an upstairs room of one of the tall, narrow buildings, and a bell jingled as someone inched open a shop door then shut it again.

"I'd not fancy living here myself," said the driver, as he handed the last of the boxes to Pip. "It's a bit creepy, isn't it? Too quiet."

"That's just because it's a Sunday," said Mr Ruskin. "It's mostly office workers who pass through here. Come Monday morning, we'll have plenty of customers."

Mr Ruskin hurried back into the dusty shop and began to tear open the cardboard boxes with great enthusiasm. Pip left him to it and went back upstairs, past the dreary sitting room and up to the set of bedrooms on the top floor. There was one with a single bed in it that didn't look too awful – it looked out over the alley instead of a brick wall – and he sat down heavily on the jangling mattress. It had been warm when they were moving their things inside, but now he shivered in his thin grey jumper. He remembered that the rest of his clothes were still in the suitcases he'd left in the car, which was still parked on Magwitch Street.

Pip grabbed the keys from where Mr Ruskin had dropped them on the kitchen counter and went back outside. It was dusk now and the alley was dark, save for a couple of old-fashioned street lights that cast a dim orange glow. He passed the pub, which was lit up, and shadowy figures were silhouetted behind the little glass squares of the mullioned windows. There was no sign of the girl or her dog.

There was a light on in the bookshop and a round-faced man with wispy grey hair was sitting at the desk, reading. Pip didn't stop, but carried on up the alley and out into Magwitch Street. It was still very quiet. A couple swept past him, arm in arm, on their way to somewhere else. Pip retrieved his bags from the car and headed back towards Elbow Alley. As he turned the corner by the gallery, he came face to face with a man standing in the shadows of the arch, smoking a cigar. It was so unexpected that Pip only just managed to hang on to his suitcases.

The man was dressed smartly, in a dark suit. His features were sharp, his cheeks sunken and his greying black hair was slicked back severely. All of this made him look intimidating, but that wasn't what made Pip stare. It was his deathly paleness. His skin was almost luminous in the twilight, as white as paper.

The man looked at Pip coldly. His pupils were huge and rimmed with red. Pip edged past him, his skin prickling, and the strong smell of tobacco caught in his throat.

The man finished the cigar, dropped it on the ground, then, to Pip's utter shock, he vanished. Pip looked around wildly, trying to figure out where the man had gone. There was a black studded door behind where he had stood, but Pip was certain that it hadn't been open. He looked up and down the alleyway, but there was no sign of the man.

One side of his brain was screaming at him, insisting that he had seen the man melt through the solid door. The other side, the logical part of him, told him it was impossible, that he was being ridiculous.

Perhaps he'd imagined it. The stress of the day, the strange surroundings, the shadows, any one of those things would be enough to make your imagination play tricks on you. But it was hard for Pip to keep telling himself that when there was the butt of the cigar lying at his feet, the tip of it still glowing, sending a wisp of smoke into the cold air.

3

The Shape in the Night

"Have some more, Pip, go on," said Mrs Ruskin, pushing the carton of seaweed-covered tofu towards him. "It's full of protein and it's so tasty."

Pip speared another chunk of tofu with his wooden fork, and stared miserably at the white lump. The seaweed made it look like something you'd find at the bottom of a rock pool. There were many words you could use to describe the tofu, Pip thought, but tasty wasn't one of them.

The Ruskins were having dinner that evening in the sitting room, around their familiar old dining table, which was too big to fit in the tiny kitchen. Everything was still untidy, with boxes heaped up and the old computers still sitting in the corner because none of them knew if they were allowed to put them into the bin or not. Mrs Ruskin had come back bright and happy, full of stories about how lovely her new department was, and bearing a large brown bag packed with takeaway meals that she'd bought from a vegan restaurant.

"I thought we'd treat ourselves," she said. "Otherwise we'd have had to order in a pizza."

Pip's mouth watered at the mention of it. For a moment, he closed his eyes and allowed himself to imagine they were sitting in front of a giant pepperoni pizza, with a delicious chewy crust, the rich tomato base smothered with melted mozzarella. Maybe there would be garlic bread, too, dripping with butter, and he'd have a can of Coke as well. It was Pip's idea of heaven.

"Pip? Are you feeling tired?" His father's voice cut through his pleasant daydream. Pip opened his eyes and surveyed his actual dinner with disgust. Aside from the tofu, there were several smelly containers of fermented vegetables and equally smelly dips; a vegetable casserole that tasted of nothing but was full of strange yellow lumps; and a watery, scratchy salad of iceberg lettuce and grapefruit. There was also a side dish of "healthy spaghetti" which was horribly misleading as it wasn't spaghetti at all, just long spirals of cold limp courgette covered in olive oil.

"I'm fine," he said, and swallowed a mouthful of the fake spaghetti, trying not to shudder as the courgette slithered wetly down his throat.

They washed up their plates, then Pip's father dragged out his laptop and began to play music – awful pop music that no one in their right minds had listened to for at least twenty years. Pip knew what was coming next, and sure enough his parents began to dance. They both had very different moves. His mother waved her arms around a lot and swayed from side to side, while his father jumped up and down in time to the music as if he was on a trampoline. When Pip was very little, he used to join in, but ever since his parents had danced in front of his entire school during a fundraising evening, he had refused to participate. He still couldn't think of that fundraising evening without feeling ill from the embarrassment of it.

"Come on, Pip," cried Mr Ruskin, out of breath and red-faced, but still springing about like a pogo stick. "Dance! We're celebrating!"

"I'm going to bed," said Pip, and climbed up the narrow staircase, his feet squelching slightly in the damp brown carpet.

He'd unpacked his suitcases and set out his things as

neatly as he could. He had wrestled his duvet and sheets onto the bed, and arranged his books on the shelves. He didn't have any posters or pictures, so his walls were still bare and white, aside from an old metal-framed mirror left by the previous tenants. Pip's collection of grey jumpers were hanging neatly on the plastic coat hangers in the wardrobe, and his three pairs of identical blue jeans were on the shelf beside them. There were lots of other clothes too, corduroy trousers like Mr Ruskin's, hand-knitted jumpers and brightly coloured socks, but Pip had stowed these away in the chest of drawers, out of sight. Deep down, he quite liked the jumpers and the socks (the canary yellow trousers were another matter) but he knew it wasn't sensible to wear them. Mrs Ruskin's hand-knitted creations weren't going to help him blend in. He didn't know what his new school would be like, or how he was going to deal with his weird new surroundings here in Elbow Alley, but he was certain of one thing: a knitted jumper with a fox on it was never going to be a good idea.

There were no curtains on the window, and his bedside lamp was still stowed away in one of the many boxes downstairs, so he got into his pyjamas by the dim light from the alleyway and climbed into the squeaky bed. He pulled his duvet up around his ears, to drown out the sounds of the pop music that was still drifting up through the floorboards, and screwed his eyes up tight, waiting for sleep to come.

In the middle of the night, Pip awoke with a start. He'd heard a crash, somewhere in the flat.

He sat up, listening intently, but everything was silent once more. Pip rolled himself back up in his duvet and tried to go back to sleep. There was still a faint light from the street coming in through the window, but it looked cloudier than he'd remembered. As Pip watched it, he realized that the mist was growing thicker. Then, with a jolt, he realized that the mist was *inside* his room.

Confused, he pushed himself up onto his elbows. The mist wasn't coming in from outside at all, but was rushing through the gap beneath his bedroom door. It had fogged over his bedroom mirror, and was forming itself into a wide swirling column that towered from the floor to the ceiling, growing steadily denser. Pip had never seen anything like it before. He watched it, fascinated. Then, to his horror, the mist began to move towards him.

Pip pressed himself against the wall, trying to get as

far away from the mist as he could. It was no use. The column kept spinning, getting closer and closer. As it neared his bed, he saw that it had a face.

The eyes and nose were empty black holes, like a skeleton's, and it had a wide gaping mouth with long teeth. The mist swayed in front of Pip like a snake, its evil face staring right at him. Then, with a rush, it swooped forwards and swallowed him up.

All he could see was billows of white cloud. He felt a terrible tugging feeling coming from inside his head and his chest, as if his insides were being sucked out by an enormous vacuum cleaner. His ears and eyes and nostrils hurt, as if something was being dragged out of them. Pip couldn't escape, or even move. He knew it was trying to take something from him, wanting to hurt him, but he was powerless to do anything to defend himself. He felt rooted to the spot.

But suddenly, it stopped. In an instant, the terrifying face vanished and the mist swirled away. It floated towards the window, seeped through the gaps in the frame and vanished as suddenly as it had come.

For a moment, Pip stared at the window in shock. His heart was pounding, and he was clammy with sweat. He took a few deep breaths, trying to steady himself.

As his panic finally cleared, he realized that he felt fine. It was as if nothing had happened.

As the minutes passed, Pip told himself that it must have been a dream. He climbed out of bed and scrabbled around in his bag for his headphones, plugging himself into the familiar sounds of an audiobook. The actor's voice was calm and steady, and Pip gradually felt himself relax. He'd imagined it – of course he had. He fell asleep with the story still playing, his headphones wedged uncomfortably in his ears.

4
The Ragged Hare

It was already light when Pip woke the next morning. He freed himself from his headphones and got dressed, pulling on the same jeans and grey jumper that he always wore. He glanced at his bedroom mirror, but the surface of it was still dull and opaque. Pip ran his hand across it, trying to wipe it clean, but somehow the glass had clouded over. He remembered the mist from the night before and shivered, then went down the corridor to brush his teeth in the mouldy, beetle-infested bathroom that smelt like a sewer. The door of his parents' room was open and their bed empty – they were already up. As he went downstairs, he heard the sound of loud unfamiliar voices coming from the sitting room. His parents were sitting on the sofa in front of the broken television set – which turned out not to be broken after all – and were watching morning TV. The tattered curtains were still drawn, so the screen was the only source of light.

Pip stood at the doorway, staring at the backs of his parents' heads in shock. He couldn't believe his eyes. He'd spent nearly thirteen years listening to his father's views on television. Mr Ruskin had refused to ever get one – yet another reason why they were considered to be so odd. Pip had spent countless hours trying to persuade his parents to buy one, but they had always said no.

"It fries your brain," Mr Ruskin would always say. "Before you know it, you'll be watching it all day long. I'd rather cut off my own toes than get a television."

Yet here he was, his toes intact, gazing raptly at the screen.

Mrs Ruskin was sitting beside him, but she was staring at her phone instead. This, too, was unusual, given that his mother usually only ever used her phone to make calls or occasionally send an email.

"Morning," said Pip. "What are you watching?"

Neither of them replied. On the screen, a chef was showing a presenter how to make chocolate-chip pancakes. Pip sat down between them on the sofa, feeling pleased and confused in equal measure.

"Don't you have to go to work?" Pip asked his mother.

She shrugged, not looking up from her phone.

"What about the antiques shop?" Pip tried his father. "You said you were going to try to open it today."

Mr Ruskin gave no sign that he'd heard him. Maybe, after all those long and boring television-free years, he was trying to make up for lost time. Whatever the reason, Pip felt that this sudden change in behaviour was probably an improvement. He settled himself back against the sofa cushions and rested his feet on a cardboard box, then glanced at his mother and father, sitting quietly on either side of him. For once, they were acting just like regular parents. This, in itself, was extremely unusual. He squashed down the niggling feeling that something was wrong, and tried to enjoy the unexpected opportunity to spend a school-free day in front of the television.

Four hours later, Pip's stomach was rumbling. His parents were still staring blankly at their screens. They hadn't moved once, even though it was a Monday and after midday. They hadn't said a single word, beyond the occasional grunt, despite Pip's repeated attempts to talk to them. Now he was not only hungry, he was becoming increasingly worried. It was as if his parents had both been given personality transplants. To begin with, it had been fun, but now it was getting creepy.

Pip got up from the sofa, and rummaged through the kitchen cupboards. They were completely empty.

"There's no food," he said. It was as if he hadn't spoken. Pip yanked open the fridge door. It was empty except for the remains of last night's dinner in the fridge. He wrinkled his nose. Although he was hungry, he wasn't *that* hungry.

"Do you want me to go shopping?" he asked. Still no answer. The situation was beginning to get ridiculous. Pip wondered if the television might be the problem, so he went over and turned it off. Mr Ruskin goggled at Pip in surprise. He looked like a goldfish. Mrs Ruskin was still absorbed in her phone and didn't seem to notice. Pip grabbed it out of her hands, and she stared up at him.

"What's the matter?" asked Pip, looking from his mother to his father. "You're acting really weirdly."

Mr Ruskin just shrugged and didn't say anything.

"I thought you'd be at work," Pip said, turning to his mother. "Yesterday you were so keen to get started, you went in on a Sunday."

"It's boring," she said, in a dull voice.

"Is this a joke?" asked Pip, desperately. "Because if it is, I've had enough of it."

They didn't say anything, just stared at him stupidly. He'd never seen them act like this before. It was deeply unnerving.

"What's happened?" Pip was shouting now, partly from frustration, partly from fear. "Tell me why you're acting like this!"

Still no reply. They were just watching him as if he was a television programme, their expressions blank and emotionless. It was as if they didn't recognize him at all. A sudden surge of horror rose inside him and he felt as if the walls were closing in. He had to get out of the stuffy flat, away from these strangers who looked like his parents. It was like being in a nightmare.

He dropped his mother's phone back onto the sofa and she immediately picked it up and started gazing at it again, as if nothing had happened. Mr Ruskin pressed a button on the remote control and the programme came back on. Pip could bear it no longer. Without even bothering to put on his coat, he ran down the stairs, two at a time, flung open the door and rushed outside. His foot connected with something solid and hairy. The thing gave a loud yelp, and before Pip could stop himself, he tripped and fell forwards, head first into the alley.

Pip hit the ground hard. He'd thrown his arms out to protect himself, and he felt a searing pain in his hands and knees as they scraped across the uneven paving stones. He lay there for a moment, dazed, but then a shadow loomed over him.

"You idiot!" it shouted. "Watch where you're going – you could have *killed* him."

He squinted up and saw it was the girl in the gold jumpsuit again. She seemed furious and was clutching her dog in her arms, which was staring at him reproachfully.

"What are you on about?" said Pip, wincing as he sat up. His hands were grazed, and his jeans were torn. His left knee was already oozing blood.

"Splodge," she said. "You fell over him."

"Sorry," said Pip. "I didn't mean to."

He turned away from her, examining his cuts, his knees still too sore for him to want to get to his feet. He hoped she'd take the hint and go away – he just wanted to be on his own. He was feeling sore and shaken, and completely fed up with this strange new place, not to mention increasingly worried about his parents. The last thing he needed was another encounter with this unfriendly girl. But even though he had his back to her, he could still feel her presence, watching him as he tried to pick out the little stones that were buried in his cut hands.

Eventually she sidled around, so she was standing in front of him.

"You're bleeding quite a lot," she said.

"I know that," said Pip shortly, not bothering to look at her.

"I'm sorry for calling you an idiot," she said eventually. "I was worried about Splodge."

She set the terrier back down on its feet and it promptly sat down beside Pip, staring solemnly up at him. The dog's eyes were almost hidden beneath its mop of hair.

"You need to clean those cuts," she said. "Can you stand up?"

"Of course I can," said Pip. "I just don't want to go back inside, that's all."

The girl still stood there, watching him.

"You don't have to hang around," he said. "I'm fine."

"Were you fighting with your parents?" she asked. "I heard you yelling through the wall."

Pip didn't answer.

"Look, if you don't want to go back home, why not come into the pub to clean yourself up? I live there, there's plasters and everything."

Pip considered it.

"All right," he said, at last, getting painfully to his feet.

"Excellent," said the girl. "I'm Fliss, by the way. Short for Felicity, but the only person who calls me that is my dad when he's annoyed with me. Which is actually quite often."

"I'm Pip."

"Short for?"

Pip flushed. He always hated this bit. He really wished he could say Philip. Philip was a good name, a sensible name, the sort of name you could say without anyone looking at you oddly. The moment he was legally able to, he was going to change his name to Philip and make everyone call him that.

"Well?" asked Fliss impatiently. "I bet it's Philip. I'm right, aren't I?"

"It's Pippin," said Pip.

"Pippin?"

"Like the apple." It was better letting her think that he'd been named after a type of apple than telling the truth, which was that Mrs Ruskin had called him after one of the hobbits from *The Lord of the Rings*. Mrs Ruskin was very keen on *The Lord of the Rings*, or at least she had been until this morning. The result of this was that Pip spent a great deal of time trying to hide the fact that he was named after a hobbit. It wasn't the sort of thing you mentioned at school.

"Oh," said Fliss. Pip waited for her to laugh, or to say something horrible, but she just pressed her lips together and said, "Well, I'm usually right about things like that. You look like a Philip."

Pip was secretly pleased, but he didn't say anything.

She led the way into the pub, Pip and Splodge following close behind. There was a sign above the door saying that The Ragged Hare had been a pub since 1627 and inside it looked as if very little had changed since then. There was a jukebox in one corner, flashing brightly coloured lights; there were green EXIT signs hung over the doors, and a fridge containing beers and bottles of wine, but apart from that the long oak bar, the dingy tables and leather-covered stools looked as if they had been there for ever.

"You really live here?" asked Pip, hardly able to believe it.

"Yep," said Fliss. Even though it was still early, there were already a couple of customers. A grey-haired woman in a long pink coat was sitting in the corner and reading a newspaper, while a pair of elderly men with greenish skin were staring miserably into their pints of beer.

"That's my dad," said Fliss, pointing at the man who was prowling up and down behind the bar, moving glasses about. Aside from a similar sort of suspicious expression, he didn't look much like his daughter – he had light skin, his eyes were an odd shade of yellowish brown, and he was thickset and muscular, as if he spent a lot of time at the gym. He raised his eyebrows when he saw them come in.

"What happened to him?" he said to Fliss, looking at Pip's knees.

"He fell over," she replied. "I'm being extremely helpful, actually. Where's the first-aid kit?"

The man gave a wolfish grin and pulled a small green plastic box out from under the counter.

"Here you go," he said. "Catch."

Fliss caught it neatly.

"Thanks," she said. "Come on, Pip."

42

The rooms upstairs might have been next door to Pip's flat, but it looked as if they belonged to another world. The low ceilings had wooden beams and the place felt cosy and warm. There was even a real fire crackling away in the hearth.

"Dad loves fires," Fliss said, seeing Pip looking at it. "He'd even have one going in summer if he had his way."

She ushered Pip into the kitchen, so he could wash his cuts under the tap. Fliss insisted on dabbing his knees and hands with disinfectant, which stung so much it made Pip's eyes water. They covered up the cuts with plasters, and Fliss pronounced him cured. While she stuffed rolls of bandages and tape back into the first-aid box, Pip looked around curiously.

"Does your whole family live up here?" he asked.

"Yes," she said. "Usually my mum's here too, but she's currently on a research trip – she's on some island off the coast of Ecuador. I wanted to go with her but it's too dangerous, apparently."

Fliss made a face, as if to suggest that her mother was being utterly unreasonable.

"What sort of research trip?" asked Pip.

"She's investigating supernatural traditions over there. She works for a university – she's always been

43

interested in stuff like that. It explains why she married my dad, I suppose."

"What do you mean?"

Pip was intrigued, but Fliss suddenly stopped talking, as if she had revealed too much.

"Anyway," she said abruptly, changing the subject. "We've got loads more space than you do. I've seen the inside of your place – it's tiny."

"It's horrible," agreed Pip.

"So, what were you and your parents arguing about?"

"It's hard to explain."

"Try me," said Fliss. "I bet it's not that difficult."

"They've been acting really strangely," burst out Pip. "They've been sitting in front of the TV all morning, doing nothing."

"So?" said Fliss. "Sounds pretty normal to me."

"But that's just it," said Pip. "It's not normal, not for them. They're usually so excited about everything and now they're just…flat. They're not themselves – something's changed overnight. It's like their personalities have vanished. I don't know what's happened."

Fliss looked uncomfortable.

"I think I do," she said. She glanced around.

"You've got to watch what you say in here," she said,

pointing to the floorboards. "Everything we say drifts down to the pub below. And some of the regulars have exceedingly good hearing. Follow me."

Fliss darted through the living room and up another flight of stairs, which led to a little attic room at the top of the house.

"This is my room," she said proudly. It was entirely covered from floor to ceiling with pictures. There were postcards, pictures cut out of magazines, old greetings cards and even scraps of fabric all pinned up together, to form one giant collage that decorated all four walls. It was clear that Fliss really liked fashion, although she also seemed keen on astronomy, given how many pictures of moons there were. There were also some pictures of a slightly younger Fliss beaming in front of what looked like an erupting volcano, accompanied by a woman with elaborately braided hair and a distinctly worried expression.

"Mum refused to let me come with her on any more expeditions after that trip," said Fliss, following Pip's gaze. "Totally unfair."

She sat down on her bed and Splodge scrambled up beside her.

"So," she began, in a businesslike tone. "When exactly

did you notice that they were acting differently?"

"Just this morning," said Pip, moving a pile of clothes from a chair so he could sit down. "Last night they were dancing about, really excited about being in London, and today they're like zombies."

"Yes, we heard the dancing," said Fliss, nodding. "We thought a herd of elephants had moved in. Your parents have terrible taste in music."

"I know that."

"The problem," said Fliss thoughtfully, "is that you lot are just ordinary people, and ordinary people don't tend to do so well in this alley."

"What do you mean, 'ordinary'?" said Pip. Fliss had clearly never met his parents.

"Haven't you got eyeballs?" asked Fliss. "You must have noticed that everyone in Elbow Alley is different."

Pip shrugged.

"I haven't really met anyone apart from you," he said. "And you seem fine."

He thought he was being nice, but Fliss seemed to swell with rage.

"I am not in the least bit ordinary," she said, sounding extraordinarily affronted. "If you knew what I actually am, you'd have probably died from terror by now."

"What are you?" asked Pip curiously.

"It's really none of your business. You'll learn that everyone in the alley keeps themselves to themselves. You have to be an insider to understand what's really going on."

"Right," said Pip. He was beginning to wonder if Fliss was completely unhinged. It was probably not a great idea to be sitting alone in an upstairs room of a strange house with someone like that.

"Well, thanks for the plasters," he said, getting to his feet.

"What?" said Fliss. "You're leaving?"

"Of course I am, if you're not going to tell me anything."

"I'm about to tell you, stupid," she said. "I'm just preparing you for it."

Pip sat back down again.

"The alley's home to people who are…unusual," she said. "Hags. Banshees. Vampires. You know, those kinds of people."

"Stop messing with me," said Pip. "It's not funny."

"I'm not!" replied Fliss indignantly. "I promise they exist. I can show you."

Pip had a sudden memory of the sinister man from

the night before, the one with the red-rimmed eyes, but he pushed the thought away firmly.

"They don't exist," he insisted.

Fliss sighed. "Just imagine for a moment that what I'm saying is completely true, that magical beings are real. Of course they'd live somewhere like this."

"Why? It's just a dingy old alley."

"Yes, but it's a dingy old alley in the middle of one of the biggest cities in the world. You can get away with anything in London. Everyone's too wrapped up in themselves to care if your skin's green or if you've got fangs. Though obviously, the only people who can get away with it are the ones who can pass themselves off as humans – if you were a centaur or a three-headed ogre, you might run into a few problems."

Fliss paused and looked expectantly at Pip, as if waiting for him to agree.

"Um, yes," said Pip, wondering how long she was going to keep the joke up. "I can see how that could be difficult."

"So, there's a few pockets of London where groups of unusual people live," continued Fliss. "Elbow Alley is one of them – the shops along here are mainly visited by magical people. And because everyone keeps themselves to themselves, you never quite know who exactly is living here. I know most of the people who run the shops, but there are loads of others who are much more secretive. And we're all pretty certain that there's a spirit snatcher in Elbow Alley."

"What's a spirit snatcher?"

"The clue's in the name," said Fliss, seriously. "It takes away human spirits – it sucks them right out of their bodies. It's happened before, every time a human comes to live in Elbow Alley. The last time was about six months ago. A family with two teenagers moved here and the whole lot of them got spirit-snatched. They only lasted a week before it happened. That was why I tried to warn you when you first arrived. I told you something extremely bad was going to happen. And it has."

Pip remembered the strange misty shape that had visited him in the night and suddenly started to believe her.

"So what exactly happened to that family?" he asked, a feeling of dread creeping across him. "They're not *dead*, are they?"

"No, not dead. But almost as bad. They completely lost their personalities – they just sat around for ages staring at the walls. They just about managed to feed themselves but that was it. Eventually some relatives of theirs came and took them away. I've no idea what happened to them."

"And you're saying that's what's happened to my parents?" said Pip in horror. "They've been…what was it?"

"Spirit-snatched. Yes, sounds like it. Sorry."

Pip stared at her, aghast, unable to believe that something quite so horrible could have happened to his parents. He had spent his whole life wishing they weren't so eccentric, but their sudden transformation was much, much worse.

"But why didn't anything happen to me?" he managed at last, still grappling to make sense of it all. "I think I saw the…spirit-snatcher thing last night. It came into my room, but it just left without doing anything."

"Depends," said Fliss. "How old are you?"

"Twelve," said Pip.

"Well, that's the reason," she said triumphantly. "They never attack anyone under the age of thirteen. It's literally impossible to spirit-snatch a child. Everyone knows that. But the moment you turn thirteen, you're up for grabs."

"But I'm thirteen in a few days!"

"Really?" Fliss looked surprised. "What date?"

"The thirty-first."

"I don't believe it." Fliss was staring at him suspiciously now, as if she thought he was tricking her. "Are you sure?"

"Of course I am!"

"I'm thirteen on the thirty-first too – on Halloween. I can't believe we have the same birthday. It's weird. Don't you think it's weird?"

"Compared to everything else you've just told me?" said Pip. "No, not really."

His mind was going very fast, trying to process the sheer strangeness of what she had told him. It would certainly explain his parents' odd behaviour, as well as the strange misty creature he had seen in his bedroom the night before. He felt himself shiver just thinking about it.

"So how can I stop it?" he said at last. "The spirit snatcher?"

Fliss shrugged.

"Leave," she said. "Like I told you."

"I can't do that," said Pip. "I've got nowhere to go. And I'm not leaving my parents like this. There has to be a way of fixing them."

"In that case, you'll need my help," said Fliss. "It's

pretty obvious you won't get anywhere on your own. You don't know anything, for a start. I'll help you find the spirit snatcher. I've always wondered who it is anyway."

"But what will we do when we find it?" asked Pip.

"Easy," said Fliss confidently. "We'll threaten to reveal its identity to everyone unless it returns your parents' spirits. Nobody likes spirit snatchers, not even magical people. That's why they take so much trouble to stay hidden."

"Isn't confronting it going to be dangerous though?"

"Not if we do it before you turn thirteen," said Fliss. "It can't touch you before then, remember?"

"You're turning thirteen on the same day as me," pointed out Pip.

"It won't go for me no matter how old I am," said Fliss confidently. "Most people in Elbow Alley are magical, and spirit snatchers only tend to prey on regular humans."

"Why won't you tell me what you are?"

"Because I've only just met you, and I don't know if mI trust you yet."

"Fine," said Pip, although he desperately wanted to find out. "Well, even if it can't take our spirits before I'm thirteen, I'm sure there's lots of other ways it can hurt us?"

"Okay, so it might be slightly dangerous," admitted Fliss impatiently. "But do you have a better plan?"

Pip was silent. Elbow Alley certainly seemed unlike anywhere else he'd ever been and something very odd had happened to his parents, but the idea of it being populated by magical beings was far-fetched, to put it mildly. Then again, it was the best explanation he had. There was also the fact that he was on his own, and here was somebody offering to help.

"Okay," he said. "Let's do it."

"Excellent," said Fliss and she grinned at him. "You'd better get ready, Pip – we're going to hunt down that spirit snatcher."

5

The Ghost and the Bookshop

Pip had promised to meet Fliss first thing the next morning. His parents were showing no sign of moving from their spot in front of the television, but they did seem to be able to use Mrs Ruskin's phone to order food online, so at least they weren't starving, judging from the pile of empty takeaway containers beside the sofa. Pip had also borrowed some money from his mother and stocked up at the nearest supermarket. For once, he'd been able to buy exactly what he liked, and he was still feeling full after his huge dinner of hamburgers and chips. It was the only positive thing about the awful situation.

He tried his best to get his parents to talk to him, but it was no use. They just sat there, doing nothing. Mrs Ruskin had already received several calls from work wondering where she was, but although she answered her phone each time, she only responded in grunts. Pip had eventually grabbed the phone off her and told them that she was so ill she couldn't even speak.

Pip was so unnerved by the change in his parents that he could hardly bear to stay in the same room as them. He felt horribly lonely – worse than if they'd left him on his own. It was as if they were empty shells, with nothing familiar left inside them at all. It was a relief to be getting out of the flat, away from their disturbing presence.

"I'm going out!" he called, as he hurried down the stairs. Neither of his parents seemed to even hear him.

Fliss was leaning against the wall opposite his front door, Splodge curled up beside her. Today she was wearing a neon pink blazer, a short, pleated skirt and clumpy trainers with gold stripes on the sides. The blazer was so bright that Mr Ruskin's corduroy suit seemed dull by comparison. Yet strangely enough, even though Pip found it extremely embarrassing to be seen with his father, he wasn't worried about being seen with Fliss. He thought it was probably because she seemed to be far better equipped to deal with whatever life might throw at her.

"Finally," said Fliss. "I thought you weren't coming."

"Shouldn't you be at school?" asked Pip, bending down to stroke Splodge. "It's a Tuesday."

"I don't go to school," said Fliss.

Pip was stunned. Even though Fliss had told him so many strange and unbelievable things, the idea of someone his age not having to go to school seemed like the most incredible thing of all.

"How come?" he said, at last.

"I haven't been in years," she replied airily. "I think Mum tried sending me once, when I was about four, but apparently I kept biting people, so they asked me to leave. I take after Dad, I suppose. So technically I'm home-schooled, but that just means Mum sits down with me whenever she can and Mr Whipple lends me some books every now and again. In fact, that's where we're going now."

"I don't want to sit in on one of your lessons," said Pip, firmly. He didn't have to start his new school until after the half-term break, and possibly not even then, if his parents stayed in their current condition.

"It's not a lesson, stupid," said Fliss. "It's a mission. We're trying to find out more about spirit snatchers. If anyone knows something about spirit snatchers it'll be Mr Whipple, since he's read practically every book in existence."

"Wait," said Pip. "You said yesterday you'd prove that what you said about Elbow Alley was true. So show me one of these magical beings you keep going on about."

"I told you, it's only the ones that can pass themselves off as humans who live here," said Fliss.

"You said you could prove it," he insisted. "If we're going to work together to help my parents, I need to know I can believe you."

"Fine," said Fliss with a sigh. "We'll call into The Pickled Trout first, then go on to the bookshop. Mr Bletchley's one of the easiest ones to spot. But don't make it too obvious you're staring at him."

Fliss, Pip and Splodge walked through the alley, ducking past a few office workers who were hurrying past, clutching paper cups of coffee. They all had headphones stuffed into their ears and were staring at their mobile phones. There was only one place in the alley they showed any interest in, and that was the tiny café, which had a long queue of people snaking out of the door. None of them so much as glanced at the other shopfronts, not even at The Pickled Trout, which stood directly opposite.

"Told you they don't notice," muttered Fliss. She pushed the door of The Pickled Trout and the bell tinkled loudly as they went in.

The smell was the first thing that Pip noticed. The air smelt sour and ripe, like sweaty old gym shoes. He wrinkled his nose, then spotted a thin frail man gliding over to them. Pip thought he'd never seen anyone quite so insubstantial. He was of middling height, almost completely colourless, his tweed suit badly faded.

"You've smelt our prize piece, I see?" he said, giving Pip a faint smile. "The Queen Mother's Cheese can be a little overwhelming to those who are not used to it."

He gestured over to the massive mouldy lump that was sitting in pride of place in the window. There was a label next to it saying it cost five thousand pounds. Pip choked, at the price as well as at the truly appalling smell.

"It was the centrepiece of her wedding banquet," said the man proudly. "By some miracle it was left untouched at the end of the night. Just think, everything else was eaten, there was not so much as a crumb left, but this colossal specimen survived in pristine condition."

"I can't imagine why," said Pip, wishing that he could hold his nose. Beside him, Fliss gave a stifled snort of laughter, which she turned into a cough. Splodge, meanwhile, seemed to be mesmerized by the smell. He was standing on his hind legs, his mouth half-open, gazing longingly up at the rancid cheese.

"Pip's just moved to Elbow Alley," said Fliss, ignoring Splodge. "I'm showing him round."

"Augustus Bletchley, at your service," said the man, and held out his hand to Pip, whose fingers seemed to slide through his grasp. "I'm the world's leading dealer of antique food."

"Antique…" Pip trailed off, confused.

"Think about it!" cried Mr Bletchley. "All manner of things are considered to be antiques. A humble foot scraper, if it's ancient enough, will be highly sought after. I believe some people collect used postage stamps. And vintage bottles of wine change hands for thousands of pounds. Why not food?"

"I suppose you're right," said Pip.

"Here, in this shop, you can see some of the most fascinating foods that have ever existed!" said Mr Bletchley, his voice high and excited.

"Look at this!" he said, pointing at a shrivelled brown lump. "That was a piece of fillet steak that King Charles I was eating just before they cut his head off. If you examine it closely you can still see his toothmarks. Over there – do you see that box? – that contains the skeleton of a trout that was caught and consumed by the highwayman Dick Turpin, shortly before he robbed the carriage of the Duke of Wellington. They found the fish's remains in a ditch, and brought them back to London to be used as evidence. And I must show you a rather lovely gravy boat that once belonged to the Archbishop of Canterbury. The gravy's still in it, although it's evaporated by now, of course. Where on earth did I put it?"

He glanced about, scanning the shelves, then hurried across the shop and began rummaging about in a large dresser with lots of drawers, opening and shutting each one in turn. Splodge seized the opportunity to make a leap for the Queen Mother's Cheese, but Fliss managed to pull him off in time.

"What's he supposed to be?" hissed Pip, nodding at the distracted Mr Bletchley. "You said it was easy to tell."

"He's a ghost, you twit," said Fliss. "You can see right through him."

Pip stared and suddenly astonishment drenched him like a bucket of icy water. Fliss was right. He could look right through Mr Bletchley's frail, faded figure and see the outlines of the shop behind him.

"How come I didn't notice it before?" he whispered.

"You weren't looking properly," muttered Fliss. "That's the problem with you lot, you never notice anything that you don't think's possible. You just see what you expect to see, not what's really there."

Mr Bletchley gave a jubilant cry and seized a small metal object.

"Here it is!" he said, rushing back to them, holding it out for them to examine. "The Archbishop of Canterbury's gravy boat! Isn't it marvellous?"

It was just a tarnished silver pot with a tarry brown mess at the bottom of it, but both Pip and Fliss were careful to give it as many compliments as they could think of, to avoid hurting Mr Bletchley's feelings. It was extraordinary to see Mr Bletchley hold it in his see-through hands and Pip wondered why it didn't fall to the ground. The more he looked at the shopkeeper, the more obvious it seemed that he was a ghost. Mr Bletchley began rattling on about the Duchess of Anglesey's fruit cake, and Fliss gave a polite cough. He broke off at once, looking mortified.

"I'm boring you," he said. "My apologies, it's just that the subject of historic food is generally so underappreciated that I can't resist talking about it when I get the chance."

"It's extremely interesting," said Fliss. "But Mr Whipple's expecting us, so we've got to go."

"Of course," said Mr Bletchley. "I understand completely. Give him my regards. Whipple's a fascinating chap, you know. Why, just two nights ago, I saw him—"

"Mr Bletchley!" interrupted Fliss.

"You must go," he said, clapping a hand to his mouth. He turned to Pip and gave him a watery smile. "It was a pleasure to meet you, young man."

He waved them out of the shop, still clasping the gravy boat to his transparent chest.

"There you go," said Fliss, once they were outside and walking briskly back down the alley. "It's all true, just like I said."

Pip was still reeling from his encounter with Mr Bletchley. It seemed unbelievable that he hadn't noticed the shopkeeper was a ghost until Fliss pointed it out. Maybe he'd come across people like that before without ever realizing.

"So everyone who lives in this alley, every single person is…"

"Yep. They're all a bit different."

"A *bit* different?" repeated Pip. "*That's* how you describe a ghost?"

"There's no point getting hung up about that," said Fliss. "You're getting distracted. You should be far more worried about the fact you're going to be spirit-snatched in less than a week. It's already spotted you, remember? You'll be top of its list by now. The moment you turn thirteen, you'll be toast."

They had arrived at Whipple & Co. Fliss darted in, Splodge at her heels. Pip followed them. As soon as he went inside, he could tell that this was an excellent bookshop. Shelves of books covered every wall from floor to ceiling and there was a rail with one of those sliding ladders that you could climb up to reach the highest rows. There were new books with brightly coloured spines, and old books with faded covers of cloth or leather. Some looked as if they were hundreds of years old, but they were all jumbled up together, arranged by subject. The subjects varied quite a bit. *Sorcery* read one of them. *Occult Objects* read another, while another one simply said *Dangerous*. That aside, the atmosphere in the bookshop was very welcoming. There were two big armchairs near the window, and between them was a table heaped high with books. An old fogged-up mirror hung above the fireplace, Persian rugs covered the floor, and a big messy desk stood at the far end of the shop.

Sitting behind it was the same elderly man Pip had seen on his first day in the alley, completely immersed in a little pink paperback called *The Romance of Milly Jane*. As they approached, he looked up and almost leaped out of his chair with surprise.

"Fliss!" he cried, hastily hiding the paperback under a pile of receipts. "Sorry, you startled me."

"This is Pip," said Fliss. "I brought him along because we're in the middle of investigating."

"How exciting," said Mr Whipple. "What are you investigating?"

"Pip's only just moved here but something's already happened to his parents," she said, lowering her voice. "They've been spirit-snatched."

"So soon?" said Mr Whipple, sounding concerned. "My dear boy, that must be terribly distressing for you. But unfortunately, there's not much you can do about it. It happens to all of the outsiders."

"It's worse than that," added Fliss. "He's going to be thirteen on the thirty-first, same as me."

"Oh dear," said Mr Whipple, casting a worried look at Pip. "That really is most unfortunate."

"There must be some way he can avoid being spirit-snatched too?" asked Fliss.

"And a way of fixing my parents?" said Pip.

Mr Whipple shook his head slowly.

"A spirit snatcher is a very powerful being. I don't believe there's anything you can do to stop it, or to restore the spirits of its victims. The only advice I can give you, Pip, is to get as far away from Elbow Alley as you can, if you truly want to avoid it."

"I can't leave until my parents decide to go," said Pip. "And I don't want them to stay like this, it's awful."

At that moment, a man appeared from the back room, carrying a stack of books. He was stocky, with longish brown hair, pale skin and a bushy beard. A deep frown was etched into his face.

"Move!" he snapped at Pip, who leaped aside at once. The man pushed roughly past without another word and began to put the books on the shelves. His shoulders were hunched and he kept his back to them, as if they weren't there at all.

"That's Julius, my assistant," said Mr Whipple, seeing Pip's surprised look. "He's not very talkative, I'm afraid."

"You can say that again," said Fliss curtly.

"I hate him," she whispered to Pip. "He's horrible. I don't know why he even works here if he's so miserable all the time."

"Fliss," said Mr Whipple, in a reproving tone. "Don't."

"Fine," she said. She folded her arms and waited until Julius had left the room before she carried on talking.

"Isn't there anything else you could tell us about spirit snatchers? You're a librus – I thought you knew everything."

She caught sight of Pip's puzzled expression.

"It means that he's able to remember every single word he's ever read," she explained. "He absorbs books. That's why he's so brainy."

"You flatter me, Fliss," said Mr Whipple, blushing. "But sadly, I can't help you – there's hardly anything written about spirit snatchers."

"So there's nothing I can do?" asked Pip. "Apart from leaving?"

"There are certain precautions you could take," said Mr Whipple thoughtfully. "An amulet, for instance, might give you some measure of protection."

"Where would I get one of those?" asked Pip.

"Penelope's shop?" suggested Mr Whipple and Fliss nodded.

"Although, Fliss, of course, is in possession of the best amulet of all," he continued.

Fliss rolled her eyes.

"I know, I know," she said in a bored voice.

"What is it?" asked Pip curiously.

"Splodge, apparently," she said. "Or so Mum keeps telling me."

"Dogs are widely believed to be the best protection against hostile forces," said Mr Whipple. "They repel them. I'm sure that's why your mother always encourages you to take Splodge with you everywhere. She knows an incredible amount about protective charms. It's remarkable really, given that she isn't magical herself. Growing up in a place like this…I can see why she'd want you to be as safe as possible."

"Splodge is about as dangerous as a doormat," said Fliss. "I love him to bits, but he's a useless guard dog."

Mr Whipple sighed.

"Fliss, you're always so *literal* about everything," he said. "It's the dog's presence that's such an effective deterrent. Why do you think so many of the humans who own galleries and antiques shops around here keep dogs? They subconsciously feel that the dog is putting off all manner of undesirable visitors – a common problem in their line of work. I've often thought about getting a dog myself."

"I wish I could get a puppy," said Pip. "But my mum's

allergic and anyway, there isn't time."

"In that case, an amulet would be your best option," said Mr Whipple.

"Mr Whipple?" said Fliss, leaning forwards. "Do you have any idea who the spirit snatcher is?"

Mr Whipple shook his head.

"I'm afraid I can't help you," he said.

"How about that girl with the really long red hair?" cried Fliss. "She's always wandering around at night – she could totally be behind it."

"Aisling?" said Mr Whipple. "No, not her. She's a banshee. She sings in nightclubs, I believe."

"Mrs Ramirez from the café?" Fliss tried again.

"She's a hag, Fliss," said Mr Whipple mildly. "You already know what she is."

"Yeah, of course," muttered Fliss.

"What about that man from the gallery at the corner?" said Pip. "The weirdly pale one who smokes cigars."

"Sir Maxim?" asked Mr Whipple. "He's quite the mystery, but really, I don't think you should start questioning our neighbours. They live here because they know they'll have some privacy. Also, it's considered rather rude to ask people what they are. You know that, Fliss."

"So you don't know what kind of magical being he is?" persisted Pip.

"No," admitted Mr Whipple. "I don't know what Sir Maxim is, but that's no reason to suspect him."

"Yes it is!" cried Fliss. She grabbed Pip's arm. "I always thought there was something sinister about him. He's only just moved here, but I've never seen him speak to anyone – of *course* it's him."

"Fliss…" warned Mr Whipple.

But Fliss took no notice. She dashed out of the shop without another word. Mr Whipple's cheerful round face was creased with alarm and he looked rather like an elderly baby with his wispy grey hair that stuck up in tufts. He stood behind his desk, clutching at a large pile of books for support, watching them helplessly.

"Sorry," said Pip. "I'd better go too."

As he raced after Fliss, he heard the quavering voice of the old bookseller calling after them, warning them to be careful.

6
Amulets

"Right," said Fliss, as soon as Pip had caught up with her. "Here's the plan. First, we find some proof that Sir Maxim is the spirit snatcher. Then, as soon as we have something on him, we'll blackmail him. Not in a bad way. We just tell him that unless he reverses whatever he did to your parents and promises to leave you alone, we'll make sure everybody knows who he is."

"Do you think people in the alley will really care?" asked Pip. "It sounds like everyone just keeps themselves to themselves."

"Nobody likes spirit snatchers," said Fliss. "Taking someone's spirit away is literally the worst thing you can do to someone. And anyway, I don't just mean here, I mean the whole world. We'll say we'll tell the newspapers, or post it on some online forums, and before he knows it, there'll be people banging down his doors wanting to tear him limb from limb."

"Isn't that a bit dangerous for everyone else though?" said Pip. "Drawing attention to Elbow Alley like that?"

"We won't have to actually go through with it," said Fliss confidently. "Just the threat of having his identity exposed will be enough. Spirit snatchers are really private, so he'll do anything to stay hidden."

"I dunno…" said Pip. "I mean, it seems like there's a lot of things that could go wrong."

Even the memory of Sir Maxim's chilling stare sent shivers down his spine. The prospect of confronting him seemed absolutely terrifying.

"Do you have any better ideas?" asked Fliss.

Pip was silent. He didn't.

"Thought not," said Fliss. "Anyway, let's get you an amulet, so you don't get killed before we have a chance to beat the spirit snatcher. Even if you're underage and he can't spirit-snatch you just yet, you'll still be in danger. I'm fine, obviously, because I've got Splodge. Also, it won't be as interested in me because I'm not a human."

"Well, what *are* you?" Pip tried again.

"Not telling," said Fliss, with a grin, and she made a beeline for Dribs & Drabs, the junk shop beside The

Pickled Trout that had captivated Mr Ruskin. The woman who had been reading the newspaper in Fliss's pub was standing behind the counter.

She was a very round sort of person. Her steely grey hair was in tight sausagey curls that came down to her chin and she wore a furry pink coat, which covered her up completely and brushed the ground. As she came towards them, Pip noticed that her feet made a funny scratching sound on the floor.

Her shop was even more cluttered inside than Pip had thought. He could see why his father had been so charmed by it – the place looked like an extreme version of Mr Ruskin's garage. Pip felt a stab of sadness as he remembered how enthusiastic his father had been about opening his new shop. It was a complete contrast to the dull man who was currently sitting in their flat, unable to take his eyes off the television.

"We're after an amulet," said Fliss. "A really strong one."

"Why?" the woman asked, looking from Fliss to Pip with avid curiosity. "And who's your new friend?"

"This is Pip," said Fliss, introducing him for the third time that morning.

"And I'm Penelope Crowley," she said. "But you can

call me Penny. Everyone does. So what do you need an amulet for?"

"He's human," said Fliss. "And he doesn't look like he'd be good in a fight."

"Fair enough," said Penny. "I know I've got a couple round here somewhere."

She vanished out of sight behind a large cabinet, and then reappeared a moment later on the other side of a mahogany dining table. She then proceeded to do a complicated sort of wiggle around three tall plant pots and her feet, invisible under her long coat, clacked loudly on the wooden floorboards. At last, she reached a glass case, whereupon she pulled out a set of keys from her coat pocket and unlocked it.

"They're in here," she said, prising open the lid, then looked back at them over her shoulder.

"What are you doing still lurking over there?" she asked. "Come over here and have a look at them, if you're interested."

Pip and Fliss began to scramble through the assault course that was Penny's shop. It was made even harder by the fact that china vases and glass goblets stood on every surface, and they all wobbled dangerously as they went by.

"Not there!" screamed Penny, as Pip brushed against a cabinet. "Watch the Ming charger – it's worth a fortune!"

Pip grabbed at the plate which was about to topple off the side. He caught it just in time.

"And control your dog!" Penny yelled at Fliss as Splodge jumped up onto a tapestry chair. "That's the last one of its kind!"

Fliss scooped Splodge into her arms and somehow, she and Pip managed to climb, squeeze and crawl through the clutter.

"I've never seen two people so clumsy," said Penny when they reached her at last. "It was like watching a pair of hippopotamuses."

"Are all of these amulets?" asked Pip, peering uncertainly at the medals and coins that were arranged in the case.

"Of course not," said Penny. "What do you think I am, an amulet collector? There's no call for them nowadays. Those three are the only amulets I have."

She pointed to three pendants. One was shaped like a beetle, one like a cat, and the third was a flat mirrored disc with some strange symbols on it.

"The cat one's the best," she said. "Very well made. It's from Ancient Egypt."

She handed it to Pip.

"Feel the weight of it – it's pure silver."

Pip wasn't sure what he should be looking for, but examined it anyway.

"It's four hundred pounds," said Penny. "A bargain at the price."

Pip's heart sank. Four hundred pounds was a fortune. There was no way he'd ever be able to get that much money.

"I can't afford it," he admitted sadly.

Penny's face fell and she scowled at him. "Give it back then," she said, and snatched it off him. "What did you come in here for, if you didn't have any money to spend? Do you think I just give things away?"

"I didn't think—" began Pip.

"No you didn't," interrupted Penny.

"But we really need an amulet," said Fliss in her best begging voice. "Pip's in an unbelievable amount of danger."

"That's not my problem, is it?" said Penny. Over on the desk, her telephone started to ring. Penny rushed over at once, moving surprisingly quickly given how much weaving and squeezing around furniture she had to do.

"Don't even think about stealing," she said, glaring at them over her shoulder. "I'm keeping my eye on you."

"We're not going to nick anything," snapped Fliss. Splodge wriggled in her arms, trying to get free, and she put him down. Penny, meanwhile, was talking away on the phone.

"It's no use," said Pip. "We might as well leave."

Then his eyes fell on Splodge, who had wandered over to a particularly ugly urn and had lifted his leg against it. A yellow puddle was forming on the floor.

"It's fine," hissed Fliss, discreetly moving the urn to cover up the mess. "It's so filthy in here, she'll never notice. But yes, it's probably time to go."

The three of them were navigating their way through the piles of furniture back towards the door when Penny put down the phone and called out to them.

"Wait!" she cried.

They froze, wondering if she'd noticed Splodge's recent incident.

"I might be able to help you after all."

She began waddling towards them, gesturing for them to come back over to the cabinet.

"Look," she said, pulling out the ugliest of the amulets, the one covered in engraved symbols with a shiny mirrored back. "This one's the cheapest. It's sixty pounds."

"We don't have sixty pounds either," said Fliss.

"I'd gathered as much," said Penny. "However, that was my sister on the phone. I've got to go and see her the day after tomorrow, and someone needs to watch over the shop. If this young man would like to do it, he can have the amulet as payment. He looks like a sensible sort, unlike you."

"I'd love to," said Pip eagerly. "Can I have the amulet now?"

"No," said Penny. "Come back on Thursday morning at nine. And don't even think about being late."

Pip nodded, but he couldn't help feeling disappointed at having to wait for so long. His birthday was on Saturday, which didn't exactly leave them much time to track down the spirit snatcher.

Penny ushered them all outside. The wind had picked up, whistling down Elbow Alley, and as Penny stood at the door, the corner of her long coat was blown back. Pip stared. Instead of feet, she had two sets of large gnarled talons. They looked a bit like a pigeon's claws but were much bigger.

Penny saw him looking and hastily rearranged her coat, hiding them from view.

"Thursday," she repeated, and retreated back inside the shop, slamming the door shut.

"Fliss," said Pip, his mouth dry. "What sort of creature is Penny?"

"She's a harpy," replied Fliss, in an unusually serious voice. "Half woman, half massive bird of prey. Whatever you do, don't upset her. Because if you do, she could tear you to pieces."

Pip was silent as they began to walk away. Elbow Alley was turning out to be even more dangerous than he'd originally thought.

7

Sir Maxim and the Rat

"Well that's the amulet sorted," said Fliss, as they made their way up the alley. "Shame you can't get it sooner. It'll mean we can't confront Sir Maxim before then."

"So why are we heading towards the gallery?" asked Pip.

"Because we can watch him, can't we?" said Fliss. "There's no time to lose. We'll gather some proof that he's the spirit snatcher, then once we've got that amulet and are as protected as possible, we'll talk to him. We'll be safe, he'll be blackmailed and before you know it, your parents will have their spirits back and everything will be sorted out."

Pip wished he shared Fliss's absolute confidence. They were passing underneath the deep archway at the top of the alley now – the buildings on either side met across it, giving it a particularly shadowy, sinister feel.

"That's the door to his house," said Fliss, pointing at the narrow black door where Pip had caught his first sight of Sir Maxim, shortly after he'd arrived in Elbow Alley. "His house is attached to the gallery on the corner – you can see they're both part of the same building – but if we stand here, we can keep sight of both entrances at the same time."

She pulled them into an alcove that was almost directly opposite the black door.

"Now we wait," she said, leaning against the damp brick wall. "Splodge, sit down."

Splodge sat himself down between them, looking faintly confused.

"Isn't he going to wonder why we're standing here?" asked Pip.

"Who? Splodge?"

"No! Sir Maxim!"

"Oh, right. No, how will he know we're here unless he comes in or out? We're in an archway – there's no windows. And if he does go somewhere, we can follow him."

They waited for hours without spotting even a glimpse of Sir Maxim. Fliss had to return home for dinner, but Pip stayed where he was, looking from one closed door to the other. He still wasn't entirely convinced by their plan, but anything seemed better than going home to that cold, dingy flat and his silent parents. It felt better to be doing something.

"Still nothing?" Fliss asked, as she returned, clutching a small cardboard container. Splodge was trotting close behind her, his eyes fixed firmly on what Fliss was carrying.

"No one's been in or out," said Pip. "Maybe he's away."

"Here," said Fliss, handing him the container, along with some wooden cutlery. "I've brought you something to eat."

Pip opened the box and got a waft of something spicy. The medley of cooked vegetables and fish looked rather similar to Mrs Ruskin's healthy recipes, which immediately made him suspicious.

"What is it?"

"Ackee and saltfish – it's a Jamaican recipe, one of Mum's favourites. She cooked about a million portions of it before she left. You should see the freezer. She knows Dad and I would only ever eat junk food otherwise. Don't make that face – it's good. Try it."

Pip took a small bite and was pleasantly surprised. He suddenly became aware of how hungry he was, and speared a fried dumpling with his fork. It was warm and comforting – exactly the sort of food you wanted on a chilly October evening. The sun had long since set, and the narrow passage was extremely dark and shadowy.

Pip finished his meal, feeling slightly guilty at preferring it to his mother's cooking, and Fliss kept watch while he wandered up to Magwitch Street in search of a recycling bin. He had to walk through several streets before he found one and had become thoroughly cold by the time he returned. The combination of the biting wind and the dropping temperature made him feel irritable and despondent. They might wait there all night and never see Sir Maxim.

He pressed himself back into the alcove, shivering in his thin navy anorak.

"It's freezing, Fliss."

"You should've worn more clothes," said Fliss. "I'm extremely warm."

She had changed when she had gone home for dinner and was now wearing a giant goose-down jacket made from a shiny silver material. Splodge was curled up against her ankles like a furry footwarmer.

"At least I blend in," said Pip defensively. "We're supposed to be keeping a low profile, remember? Why did you wear a silver jacket of all things? You stick out like a sore thumb."

"Like a sore *what*?"

"It's an expression."

"Well, it's a stupid one. Anyway, I'd rather stand out than look as dull as you do. I've never seen you wear anything but that mangy grey jumper and jeans. Do you even have any other clothes? You couldn't dress more boringly if you tried."

She stared at him and must have read something of the truth in his face, because she shook her head in disbelief.

"That's why you wear the same thing every day, isn't it?" she said. "You actually *want* to look boring."

"I'm just trying to fit in!"

"That's pathetic. I can't think of anything worse than fitting in."

"It's different for you," said Pip, who was beginning to feel annoyed at Fliss. She didn't have to go to school, and she didn't have parents like his, so what did she know about it? Fliss lived in an alley full of harpies and ghosts, so she could be as peculiar as she liked without having to worry about the consequences. "You don't get it."

Fliss opened her mouth, about to make some furious reply, when they heard a match strike. Sir Maxim had appeared in the alley, as if from thin air, and was lighting a cigar. Pip, Fliss and even Splodge all froze, pressed into the alcove, hardly daring to breathe.

Sir Maxim puffed away on the cigar, sending clouds of smoke billowing around his sleek black hair, then began to stride away, up through the archway and down Magwitch Street. Pip and Fliss followed him, as quietly as they could, their argument forgotten. Sir Maxim walked quickly, first down one road then the next, and they soon lost track of where they were going. He turned into a poorly lit street, where nearly all the houses had black, empty windows, and the only sound was the hum of traffic from a nearby road. Halfway down it, Sir Maxim stopped abruptly, so that Fliss and Pip skidded to a halt a few steps behind him.

"Why, may I ask, are you two following me?" he said, as he turned around. His eyes gleamed with a terrifying coldness.

Fliss and Pip began to back away from him, as he came slowly towards them.

"We weren't," said Fliss.

"Don't lie to me," said Sir Maxim. "You were waiting in the alley. I saw you. You've been trailing me ever since."

"Let's run for it," muttered Pip to Fliss.

They turned, but Sir Maxim was somehow again standing in front of them, blocking their way.

"The street is a dead end," he said. "There's no point running. I can always catch you."

Pip felt colder than ever as they both stared up at the tall figure of Sir Maxim, who was even more terrifying up close. Even in the semi-darkness they could see the red rims of his eyes. Pip wished that some of the lights were on in the windows. He prayed that a passer-by would appear, but the place was completely deserted. He knew there was no point in calling out, because no one was there to hear them.

"Now tell me," Sir Maxim said again, his voice dangerously calm. "Why were you following me?"

There was a long pause. It felt like Sir Maxim's eyes were burning into theirs. Pip suddenly wondered if Fliss was right about them not being able to be spirit-snatched until they were thirteen. What if he attacked them both, there and then? All they had to protect them was Splodge, and right now the dog was standing nervously behind them, his nose buried in Pip's trouser leg.

"I wanted to ask your advice," Fliss blurted out at last. "I live just down the street from you – my dad's the landlord of The Ragged Hare – and I want to start my own gallery too, when I'm older, because I love art and fashion. And yours looks like the best. I wanted to ask you about it. I made Pip come along with me because I was too scared to go by myself."

Pip had to hand it to Fliss – she was very good at lying. She genuinely looked as if she meant every word.

"But why would you wait outside?" asked Sir Maxim, a frown creasing his pale face. "You could have just rung the bell. Or telephoned. Or emailed, for that matter. The gallery has an excellent website with all of our contact details."

"Yes," said Fliss. "That might have been a better idea. I was nervous – I wasn't thinking clearly. I thought I should ask you in person. I'm sorry for bothering you."

"No matter," said Sir Maxim, curtly. "The gallery is having an exhibition opening on Thursday evening. If you're so keen, perhaps you should come along."

"Both of us?" asked Pip.

"If you like. There will be plenty of other people attending – two more will make no difference. There's only one condition."

"What?" asked Fliss eagerly. "Do you want us to help?"

"That won't be necessary," said Sir Maxim, holding up his hand as if to ward off Fliss's enthusiasm. "No, all I ask is that you leave me in peace. I do not like being followed. Please refrain from doing so again. Goodnight."

And with that, he stalked off. They watched him vanish around the corner, then turned to each other in amazement.

"How lucky was that?" said Pip. "I thought we were done for, when he cornered us."

"That's thanks to my excellent improvisation skills," said Fliss. "This evening couldn't have gone any better. All we need to do is show up on Thursday, wait until no one's looking, then nip through to his house and have a poke round while he's distracted in the gallery. You'll have your amulet by then, in case things get nasty, and I'll bring Splodge. Couldn't be simpler."

Relief made them light-headed, and they started to retrace their steps, still talking about their narrow escape. It was only when Splodge let out a low growl that they realized a rat was scurrying along behind them.

"It's all right, Splodge," said Fliss, and pulled at his lead. "Come on."

But when Pip looked over his shoulder a few minutes later, the rat was still there.

"Scram!" he said, taking a step towards it, and the rat scuttled off at once.

"It was following us," said Pip.

"Don't be stupid," said Fliss. "You're getting paranoid. It was just a rat."

But Pip wasn't so sure. He remembered that he had also seen a rat watching him the first day they had come to the alley. There was something odd about it. He told Fliss, but she wasn't impressed.

"Strange stuff happens around here all the time," she said. "You're just not used to it yet."

Pip glanced over his shoulder again, still unable to shake the feeling that someone was watching him. Fliss made a face at him.

"Stop looking so worried," she said. "Come Thursday, we'll find all the proof we need that Sir Maxim's the spirit snatcher. And once we've done that, the rest will be easy, you'll see – we'll be able to get your parents back to normal and you'll all be safe. So cheer up – we should be celebrating."

8

The Spirit Snatcher
Strikes Again

On Wednesday morning, Pip was in the middle of a pleasant dream in which his parents had never moved to Elbow Alley at all, but had gone to a tropical island where it was permanently warm and sunny and nothing ever happened. He was just lying on a sandy beach, listening to the waves, when he became aware of a buzzing noise. At first, he thought it might be a swarm of exotic bees, but then he woke up and the buzzing kept going.

He opened his eyes blearily and realized that his mobile phone, which had fallen down the side of his bed, was vibrating. Someone was trying to call him. He stuck his arm into the gap between his mattress and the wall, and eventually found his phone. There were fifteen missed calls on it, all from the same unknown number. The only people who ever rang him were his parents, and they weren't in a fit state to be calling anyone. Even as he looked at the screen, it began to ring again. Pip answered it.

"Hello?" he said, puzzled.

"At last!" Fliss's voice crackled into his ear. "I thought you were never going to pick up."

"How do you have my number?" asked Pip.

"You gave it to me. In case of emergencies, remember? Anyway, it's quite nice to have someone my own age to talk to."

"Right," agreed Pip, rubbing his eyes sleepily. "But couldn't you have waited until later?"

"No I couldn't," cried Fliss. "The spirit snatcher's attacked someone else – it got Mr Bletchley. Everyone in the alley's talking about it."

"Mr Bletchley? But he's a ghost!"

"Exactly!" said Fliss. "It's unheard of. Usually a spirit snatcher would only ever prey on humans."

Pip's phone bleeped as the battery sign flashed red.

"Fliss, my phone's about to die."

"Come over to his shop then," she said. "Hurry."

She hung up. Pip scrambled out of bed, shivering in the icy morning air. He threw on his usual uniform, but it was too cold to wear his thin grey jumper, so he pulled open his chest of drawers and grabbed a hand-knitted one. It was striped green and white and one arm was slightly longer than the other, but it was thick and warm. He struggled into it, and pulled on a pair of green woollen socks too, for good measure. His mirror was still clouded over, so he had no idea what he looked like. Pip reflected that this was probably a good thing.

He ran downstairs, pausing to pull open the sitting-room curtains and sweep the mountain of takeaway boxes into the bin. His parents had practically taken root on the sofa.

"You'll be feeling like yourselves again soon," he said to his mother and father. "I'm working on it."

But they didn't answer. They didn't even look at him. If anything, they seemed to be getting worse.

Pip ran down the stairs, shoved his feet into his shoes and raced outside. He dodged past Julius, Mr Whipple's surly assistant, who was standing in the middle of the street just outside the bookshop, watching the growing crowd of locals who were gathering inside Mr Bletchley's shop. The door stood open, but it was so busy that Pip had to push his way in. He spotted Penny, who was wailing loudly and gave no sign that she recognized him. She was weeping onto Mr Whipple's shoulder – the old bookseller looked in danger of collapsing under her weight. He saw Mrs Ramirez from the café across the street – Fliss had pointed her out to him the day before. She was hovering in the doorway, clearly torn between the developing drama and the growing queue of impatient customers who were waiting for their morning coffee. An unfamiliar greasy-haired couple dressed entirely in black velvet were lurking beside a cabinet, wringing their hands. The only creature who seemed completely calm was Splodge, who was sprawled out on the floor, fast asleep, his nose twitching.

As he looked around for Fliss, he saw the faintest outline of Mr Bletchley, still standing behind the counter. He seemed to be flickering, like a candle that was about to go out. Before, you had to look closely to see that he was a ghost, but now you could easily walk through him. He was barely there at all. He wasn't speaking or moving, just staring sadly straight ahead of him, his expression as fixed as a photograph.

"It's horrible, isn't it?" Fliss had appeared at his side. "Poor Mr Bletchley."

"But what's wrong with him?" said Pip. "That's nothing like what happened to my parents. Are you sure it was the spirit snatcher?"

"Of course it was!" cried Penny and she rounded on them, still dabbing at her eyes with a handkerchief. "A ghost is mostly spirit, you silly boy, so if you take that away there's hardly anything left. Of course it would be worse for him than if he was alive."

Mr Whipple was looking extremely worried.

"Excuse us a moment, Penny," he said, and he drew Fliss and Pip into the only empty corner in the shop, the one that was uncomfortably close to the Queen Mother's Cheese.

"If you're still on the hunt for a spirit snatcher, I'd strongly recommend you stop," he said to them, keeping his voice low.

"But we're so close," said Fliss. "And this proves it even more."

"What do you mean?" asked Mr Whipple.

"Sir Maxim's house is right next door, isn't it?" said Fliss. "Mr Bletchley could have spotted something. Maybe that's why he was spirit-snatched."

"Don't, Fliss," pleaded Mr Whipple. "You really shouldn't be meddling. You're putting yourselves and everyone else in real danger."

"But what else are we supposed to do?" asked Pip. "What about my parents?"

"It's extremely unlikely you're going to be able to get them back to how they were before, Pip," said Mr Whipple gently. "I've never heard of anyone being able to undo the work of a spirit snatcher. It's impossible. And it would be absurdly dangerous to even try."

Pip didn't say anything. Neither did Fliss. They just gazed stubbornly at the bookseller, until Mr Whipple gave a sigh.

"I can see that nothing I say is going to stop you. But please, for you own sakes, be careful."

In the distance came the sound of church bells striking the hour. Mr Whipple looked startled and checked his watch.

"I must open up the bookshop," he said. "I should have done it an hour ago."

"Can't Julius do it?" asked Pip. "He's there already – I saw him earlier."

"I suppose he could," admitted Mr Whipple. "For some reason, I always feel as if I have to keep an eye on him. It's just me being silly, of course. I fuss too much."

He looked nervously from Fliss to Pip. It almost seemed as if Mr Whipple was afraid of his own assistant.

"Look after yourselves," he said, then hurried away.

* * *

No one seemed to know what to do with Mr Bletchley. They couldn't move him – when Pip and Fliss tried, their hands slipped right through his faint outline. Eventually Penny, who was a friend of Mr Bletchley and had a spare key, announced that she would lock up The Pickled Trout and check on Mr Bletchley once a day. She began to shoo them all outside.

"I still don't get why the spirit snatcher would go for Mr Bletchley," Pip muttered, as they got carried along in the departing crowd.

"Like I said, maybe he knew something," said Fliss. "Or got in its way. Or maybe the spirit snatcher just couldn't bear that awful smell any more – it really does stink in there, doesn't it?"

"Psst," came a voice, so close Pip felt clammy breath tickle his ear. He whipped around, and saw that the velvet-clad man from the shop was hovering close behind him. He looked like a mole, with big white hands, small squinting eyes and a long fleshy nose that turned up at the end. His hair was long and tied with a velvet ribbon, and he was small, barely the same height as Pip.

"I heard you talking in the shop," he said. He leaned forwards and whispered in Pip's ear again. "About the spirit snatcher," he breathed.

"Er, yes," said Pip, with a shudder.

"And I saw you both the other day too, you was watching Sir Maxim's place," he continued.

"So?" said Fliss. She folded her arms and glared at him.

"Come inside," said the man, and pointed at a shop that Pip had not noticed before. *Past Caring* was written above it in faded gold letters. The outside of it was painted black and dark velvet curtains hung across the windows so you couldn't see what was inside. If Pip had to guess at what kind of business it was, he would have said it was a funeral home.

It gave him the chills. Fliss clearly felt the same way because she bent down and picked up Splodge, tucking him under her arm before they followed the strange little man inside.

If the outside looked funereal, it was nothing compared to the interior. It was draped in black and several gravestones were propped up on either side of the fireplace. There were death masks hung upon the walls, along with marble memorial tablets and tarnished silver urns.

"Have you been in here before?" Pip asked Fliss in a low voice, and she shook her head.

"No," she hissed back. "The owners are really creepy – I've always stayed away."

"Do you like it?" said the man, in that same whispery tone he had used before.

"It's very…interesting," said Pip. "But who are you? I don't think we've met."

"Course we've not met," said the man. "I'm Seymour Graves and this is my wife Deathly." He gestured to the woman who had been with him in The Pickled Trout, who was now standing in the gloom watching them. She and her husband were almost identical – they looked like twins.

"It's wonderful, isn't it?" she said, sounding oddly elated. "About Augustus. To have died once is a privilege, but to be so close to dying twice—"

"What *is* this place?" Fliss interrupted. She was peering at the gruesome displays, looking half-disgusted and half-fascinated. Deathly glared at her.

"It's our business, of course," she said. "Anything to do with mourning, that's what we sell. Come and look."

She beckoned them over to the large glass display cabinets that were arranged above the fireplace. They were full of jewellery, most of it made from human hair. There were rings engraved with names, with graves, with weeping angels. There were strands of hair – golden hair, brown hair, black hair and grey – plaited and knotted into intricate shapes, embalmed in resin and enamel, and made into pendants, rings and brooches. Pip felt a little queasy at seeing so much of it massed together, or perhaps he was feeling sick at the rapturous expression on Deathly's face.

"Are you hungry?" Seymour had sidled up to Pip again, whispering right into his ear. Pip twisted away from him, feeling uncomfortable.

"What about you?" said Seymour, turning to Fliss instead. "We're about to have breakfast."

"It's only rats," said Deathly, pointing to a couple of dead rodents lying on the counter. "Or woodlice. There's lots of woodlice but you'll have to squash them first and leave them for a bit. You won't want to eat them fresh."

"I'm okay," said Fliss, shaking her head. Deathly, who seemed to have taken a shine to Pip, picked up one of the rats by its tail and dangled it in front of him.

"You'll have a nice bit of rat though?" she said, in a wheedling voice.

"I've already eaten," Pip lied. Deathly looked a little offended and gave the rat to her husband instead. She picked up the other one and started to chew on its ear with pointed white teeth. Pip watched in horror, wondering what on earth this strange couple *were*.

"So what did you want to tell us?" said Pip, turning to Seymour and immediately wishing he hadn't. Seymour had bitten the head off his rat and was chewing with his mouth open.

"Umble," said Seymour. "Klop. Rumbit."

Pip and Fliss were mystified.

Seymour swallowed, then cleared his throat.

"I said," he repeated, "we know things. Lots of things. You're after the spirit snatcher, aren't you?"

"Do you know who it is?" asked Pip.

"Remember what we said, Seymour," said Deathly, giving her husband a stern look. "The plan."

"Yes, yes," said Seymour, and he turned back to Fliss and Pip.

"I can't tell you right now," he said. "But we can show you."

He took another mouthful of rat and chewed gloomily.

"I hate rats," he said.

"Why eat them, then?" asked Fliss, sounding exasperated.

"Because rats is all we have," snapped Deathly, looking extremely offended. "Rats, woodlice, mice, pigeons."

"A fox, sometimes," said Seymour. "If it gets squashed on the road."

"I think she meant, why not eat normal food?" said Pip as politely as he could. Fliss and Deathly were glaring at each other.

"Because we're ghouls," replied Deathly. She pulled a maggot from her rat, then rolled it between her fingers. "And ghouls eat flesh. The more rotten it is, the better."

"It used to be different," said Seymour. "Two, three, four hundred years ago, London was the best place to be a ghoul. Bodies everywhere you looked. Sometimes they was just left on the street."

"It's not like that now," said Deathly. "We haven't had so much as a sniff at a proper decaying corpse since the war. There's not even an open graveyard for miles round. Just old ones, full of dry bones with not a scrap of meat on them."

"It's all changed," moaned Seymour. "No more crunching, no more biting. Just sitting at the side of a road, waiting for a pigeon to be run over."

"It's demeaning," agreed his wife. She dropped the rat onto the ground and kicked it across the floor, then slumped down beside a headstone, moaning to herself. Fliss discreetly rolled her eyes at Pip.

"Can't you just go to the supermarket?" she suggested.

Deathly let out a terrible wail.

"Never!" she gurgled. "Too many lights, too many people, too many *beeps*."

"You could always order online, then."

Deathly looked at Fliss with an utterly blank expression. It was clear that she wasn't familiar with the internet.

"What did you want to show us, anyway?" asked Pip, who was becoming increasingly keen to leave the shop and get as far away as possible from its unsavoury inhabitants.

"Can't tell you now – we need to get it ready, don't we?" said Seymour, sucking the rat's tail into his mouth like a strand of spaghetti. "But it'll be worth it. We know everything you want to find out."

"You've got proof?" asked Pip. "Of who the spirit snatcher is?"

"Oh yes," said Deathly, breaking off her moaning and looking up at them. "Meet us in St Sepulchre's, the old church on Dullmarsh Street, tomorrow at midnight. We'll tell you all about it."

"Tomorrow's the night of the exhibition," said Fliss, giving Pip a meaningful look.

"Can't you just tell us now?" asked Pip, but both ghouls shook their heads violently.

"Has to be there," said Seymour. "It'll be worth it, though, we promise."

"Yes," said Deathly, grinning weirdly. "We promise."

"Okay," said Fliss. "Tomorrow at midnight it is. See you then."

She and Pip hurried out of the gloomy shop, blinking as their eyes adjusted to the daylight.

"Urgh," said Fliss, as soon as they were out of earshot of the velvet curtains. "Those two are disgusting."

"We're not really going to meet them, are we?" asked Pip. "I don't trust them."

"If we can prove Sir Maxim's the spirit snatcher, we won't have to."

9

Breakages

Thursday morning dawned and Pip awoke with a feeling that the plan was finally coming together. He was going to get the amulet, then hopefully they would manage to find some proof that Sir Maxim was the spirit snatcher. Once they'd done that, it was just a matter of speaking to the gallery owner and somehow making him return the spirits he had stolen and leave everyone in Elbow Alley alone. He tried his best not to think about all the things that could go wrong, especially as he was getting increasingly worried about what would happen if his parents stayed in their current state. Mrs Ruskin would lose her job, they wouldn't be able to pay the rent and they'd end up homeless. And if he ended up having his spirit taken too – his birthday was the day after tomorrow, after all – then the entire family would be completely helpless. Just thinking about it made Pip's insides twist in fear. He pushed the unpleasant thought firmly to the back of his mind.

"I'm going to look after that shop you liked," he said to his father. "It was called Dribs & Drabs, remember? Why don't you come with me?"

But his father simply continued to stare at the television, while Mrs Ruskin sat beside him, looking equally comatose.

"Please," tried Pip, and he seized hold of his father's arm. "Just for a couple of hours – you should get out of the house."

He tugged at his father's sleeve, trying to haul him to his feet, but it was impossible.

"No," Mr Ruskin said simply, and sank back down into his seat.

Pip gave up and left them to it. He arrived at Dribs & Drabs promptly, at five minutes to nine, and met Penny coming out of Mr Bletchley's shop.

"He's no better," she said. "If anything, I think he's getting fainter."

Pip could tell she was flustered from the way she opened her shop door, stabbing at the lock with the key, her hand shaking.

"I'm thinking of leaving Elbow Alley," Penny said as they went inside. "Something's not right around here."

Pip looked around at the shop, which seemed even more cluttered and chaotic than it had done on Wednesday.

"What am I supposed to do?" he asked, feeling slightly overwhelmed.

"It's quite simple," said Penny, rootling about the counter and seizing a large blue handbag. "If anyone comes in, watch that they don't steal anything. The prices for everything are in this ledger here, and if a customer wants to buy something, make them pay cash. That's all there is to it. I'll be back at six."

And with that, she clacked out of the shop, leaving Pip alone. He wandered about the shop, trying not to knock anything over, and had another look at the amulet. The bell above the door tinkled and Pip put on his most professional expression, ready to greet a customer. Instead, Deathly sidled in, carrying a brown-paper package.

"I've brought you a present," she said, offering it to Pip. "Fatten you up a bit. You're very thin, aren't you?"

Pip prodded it, and his finger struck something sharp and spiky.

"Ouch!" he cried, drawing away his hand. A brown spine, sharp as a needle, was poking through the paper. "What is it?"

"A lovely big hedgehog," she said. "They're good for eating, if you go for the soft bits. It's only a little bit squashed."

"I really don't want a…"

"Keep it," she said insistently. "It's a present. Delicious."

"Thanks," he said, giving in.

"We'll see you tonight," she said, in that same doleful tone. "At St Sepulchre's at the stroke of midnight. You won't forget?"

"Of course not," said Pip, secretly praying that they wouldn't have to go there. Deathly gave a satisfied nod and drifted out of the shop.

Fliss came in moments later, Splodge at her heels.

"Was that Deathly leaving just now?" she asked. "What was she after?"

"She brought me a dead hedgehog," replied Pip. "And she wanted to remind me about tonight."

"Urgh," said Fliss, inspecting the parcel. "What are you going to do with it?"

"Well I'm not going to eat it, that's for sure," replied

Pip, pushing the package away from him. "Are we still on for the exhibition?"

"Yes, of course," replied Fliss. "I think we should—"

There was a loud crash of breaking china, and Splodge rushed out from underneath a table, looking alarmed. Pip hurried forwards and saw one of Penny's precious vases, smashed into pieces.

"Splodge!" cried Pip.

"It's not his fault," said Fliss, cradling the terrier protectively. "It's this useless shop – of course things are going to get broken if they're stuck in such stupid places."

"I bet he was trying to pee on it again," muttered Pip, as he got down on to his hands and knees and began to gather up the broken shards of china.

"Can you find any glue?" he asked desperately, looking up at Fliss. "Maybe we can stick it back together."

He cleared a space on the messy desk, tossing a stack of papers to the floor and putting Deathly's package on one of the chairs. Then he began to arrange the china fragments on the table, trying to form it back into a vase.

"It's like you're trying to do a jigsaw puzzle with half the pieces missing," said Fliss. She picked up another shard that had landed close to her feet. "You'll never manage to put it back together again."

"So what am I supposed to do then?" said Pip, exasperated. "We need to get the amulet – there's no way she's going to give it to me if something's been broken."

"Just hide it," advised Fliss. "I bet she won't notice it's missing. Look at how much stuff's in here."

Pip rummaged about under the desk and found a plastic bag. He swept the pieces into it, then popped the entire bag into one of the big plant pots.

"I'll tell her once I've got the amulet," he said. "I'll call in tomorrow and confess, offer to work a few more days to make it up to her."

"Just make sure you're at a safe distance when you come clean," Fliss advised. "She's a harpy, remember?"

Pip was unable to settle for the rest of the day. Only one person came in – a tourist who had clearly got lost – and she hastily backed out again without even returning Pip's greeting. Fliss had left shortly after the vase incident, and he had promised to call in to The Ragged Hare once he had the amulet, so they could both walk over to the exhibition. That left him with plenty of time to imagine how Penny would react when he told her about the accident. When she finally arrived back, half an hour late, he was waiting by the case containing the amulets, keen to get out of there before she realized anything was wrong.

"What's the matter with you?" said Penny suspiciously. "Why are you lurking over there and not behind the till?"

She had returned in a filthy mood and had stamped into the shop, looking ruffled and irritable.

"I've got to go," said Pip. "I'm late."

"What on earth is so important?" said Penny rudely.

"Sir Maxim invited me and Fliss to an opening this evening and it's already started," he explained.

"Ooh, Sir Maxim invited you to something, did he?" said Penny, scowling at him. "Doesn't invite anyone else, but you and Fliss, on the other hand…"

"Can I have my amulet now?" asked Pip, taking it out of the glass case and turning it about in his hand. "I really need it."

"No, you can't," she said. "I've changed my mind."

"What?" cried Pip.

"You'll have to do another day in the shop tomorrow, then maybe I'll let you have it."

"That's not fair!" he said indignantly. "You promised."

"So?" she said nastily, and began pulling down the shutters of the large front window. "Life's not fair. You should get used to it."

Pip only just managed to stop himself from making a furious retort. Instead, he took a deep breath and decided to beg.

"Please can I have the amulet?" he said. "I'll work in the shop tomorrow, I'll work here all next week if I have to, if you'll just let me have it tonight."

"No," she said. "Come back tomorrow, then we'll see. Now put it back in the case and get out of here."

She turned away and carried on tugging at the rusty shutters. Pip looked down at the amulet in his hand. Their whole plan depended on Pip having the amulet tonight – there was no way he could confront Sir Maxim without some sort of protection. He was turning thirteen the day after tomorrow, so he couldn't afford to wait. Pip had never stolen anything in his life, but at that moment, something took hold of him. Instead of putting the amulet back into the case, he slipped it into his pocket, then dodged his way through the shop, said goodbye to Penny, and left. As he walked down the alleyway towards The Ragged Hare, a terrible screech tore through the air. It was Penny. Without looking behind him, Pip sprinted for the pub, and almost dived through the door.

"Where have you been?" cried Fliss. She looked smarter than usual in a long silk dress, although she had paired it with a sturdy pair of boots and her embroidered denim jacket. "We should've been there by now."

"I've got to hide," said Pip, looking wildly around. He raced behind the bar and ducked down behind it, and Fliss's father, who was drying glasses, stared at him in surprise.

"Penny's after me," he croaked, in explanation. "You can hear her screaming from here."

"Was it the vase?" said Fliss, pushing open the door and grinning as she heard Penny's yells echoing down the alley.

"Could have been," said Pip. "But I think it was the amulet. She changed her mind about giving it to me, so I took it."

Fliss gave a low whistle. "Good work," she said. "I wouldn't have thought it of you."

"You've stolen something?" growled Mr Wells, from the other end of the bar. He gave Pip a terrifyingly stern frown.

"No, of course he hasn't," said Fliss impatiently. "Penny's been trying to cheat us, that's all. But you can't stay here, we've got to get to the exhibition."

"I can't walk past Dribs & Drabs again," said Pip. "She'll see me."

"Well, lucky for you I'm extremely good at creating diversions," said Fliss in a low voice so her father couldn't hear. "I'll go into the shop and see what's the matter, then you can slip past while she's talking to me."

"She knows we're going to the exhibition together," said Pip. "She might go for you too."

"I can look after myself," said Fliss, calmly. "Give me a couple of minutes' head start, then head for the gallery. I'll meet you outside."

Fliss marched out of the pub, dragging Splodge behind her. Pip waited, conscious that Mr Wells was still watching him suspiciously. After a few minutes, Pip poked his head out of the door and peered down the alley. It was empty. He began to walk quietly up the street and ducked down low as he passed the shop. The door stood wide open, so he could hear everything. Penny was still screeching and Fliss was making soothing noises.

He rounded the corner of the alley and went up to the gallery. It was lit up with extra lights, people milled about outside and for once the main door stood open. A pale girl with a clipboard was standing in the entrance. It all looked incredibly smart and Pip felt very out of place as he hovered by the railings outside in his navy anorak, waiting for Fliss. At last she appeared, and when she caught sight of him, she burst into peals of laughter.

"What happened?" said Pip, hurrying forwards. She shook her head, unable to speak, and Splodge looked solemnly up at her.

"It was the amulet, wasn't it?" he cried. "She wants it back."

But Fliss just made a choking noise and shook her head once more.

"The vase?" Pip tried again.

"Worse," she croaked, as she was overwhelmed by another fit of laughter.

"Tell me!" said Pip. "Is it something else? She's not angry at me?"

"Oh, Penny's absolutely furious at you," she said weakly, wiping tears from her eyes. "You're not going to believe it, but she sat on Deathly's hedgehog."

10

The Grand Exhibition

"She's probably going to kill you," said Fliss. "The hedgehog thing was bad enough – she thinks you put it on her chair on purpose – but then she spotted the plastic bag in the bottom of that plant pot just as I was leaving. And it's only a matter of time before she sees the amulet's missing."

"I thought the whole point of getting the amulet was so it would protect me against magical creatures," Pip groaned.

"Well if it was her amulet in the first place, I don't think it's going to be much use against her. But we can work out how to calm down an angry harpy later. We've got more important things to do."

They were standing inside Sir Maxim's gallery, huddled in a corner. The inside of the gallery was painted the same deep red as the exterior, and the only lights in the room were the ones that shone on the oil paintings that were arranged on the walls. It made it hard to see the faces of the people who were milling about the shadowy room. A few waiters circled about, topping up the glasses of champagne and offering plates of canapés.

"We need to get down to the far end," said Fliss, standing on tiptoes and peering across the room. "There's a door down there – I bet it leads into his house."

They began to fight their way through the crowd, carefully avoiding Sir Maxim, who was standing in the middle of the room, surrounded by a group of admirers.

"They're nearly all humans," said Fliss, in a superior sort of voice.

"How can you tell?" asked Pip.

"I just can," she said. "It's easy if you've grown up in a place like Elbow Alley. And I'm actually half-human too, so I know what I'm looking for."

"So does that mean one of your parents is magical?" asked Pip, who was still dying to know what Fliss's secret powers were.

"Well my mum is fully human, if you hadn't already guessed. Even though she spends all her time hunting down supernatural stuff. Dad's the one you've got to watch out for."

"What is he?" asked Pip eagerly.

"Nope, not telling," said Fliss.

"But you must have inherited his magical powers, or whatever he has," said Pip, trying to draw it out of her.

At this, Fliss rounded on him. "If you keep on asking, I'm not going to help you any more."

"Fine," said Pip. "I don't care anyway."

This was a lie of course. He was more curious than ever, but he knew this wasn't the time to push it.

They finally reached the door, and to their dismay, they saw one of the gallery assistants was standing guard right in front of it, making sure that no one went in.

"She'll have to leave eventually," said Fliss, as they watched the door from a safe distance. "Maybe we could slip past her."

"We'll be noticed," said Pip. "Haven't you spotted that people are looking at us? We're the only ones in here with a dog."

"I had to bring Splodge," said Fliss defensively. "We need him to protect us, remember?"

Pip checked his pocket, just to make sure that the amulet was still safely in there. It was, which made him feel better about breaking into Sir Maxim's house.

"Maybe we can distract her," said Pip, as an idea

occurred to him. He watched as one of the waiters came towards them, twirling about theatrically and holding out an enormous plate of mouth-watering canapés. Just as the waiter swung round, Pip reached out as if he was going to take one, and knocked the giant silver plate with his hand. The waiter jumped, then tried to regain his balance, but it was too late. The plate slipped out of his hands and hit the floor with a crash, sending food flying everywhere. Several people screamed and the assistant guarding the door rushed forwards to help. Pip melted backwards, into the crowd.

"Not bad," said Fliss, grinning at him. Within seconds they had crossed the room and slipped through the door, Splodge at their heels, unnoticed by anyone.

They found themselves in a narrow corridor. At the end of it was another door, the key still in the lock. They opened it and darted through, shutting it quickly behind them.

"We did it," whispered Fliss, as she gazed around. "We're in Sir Maxim's house."

They were in a large chilly hall, with a marble floor and a high ceiling. All the windows were boarded up, which struck Pip as strange. A chandelier hung from the ceiling, throwing a dim flickering light across the room.

Fliss was opening each of the doors that stood around the hall, peering inside each one.

"What are we supposed to be looking for?" asked Pip.

"I'm not sure," admitted Fliss. "But there must be something. Papers. Books. A diary. Or what about the stolen spirits? Do you think that the spirit snatcher absorbs them or keeps them somewhere?"

"I don't want to think about it," said Pip, feeling sick at the thought of what might have happened to his parents' spirits. "Let's split up, since there's so many rooms. The quicker we find something, the better."

"Good idea," said Fliss. "You've got your amulet?"

Pip nodded.

Fliss and Splodge went through the nearest door, into an ornate drawing room, while Pip tried the handle of the one beside it. He found himself in the dining room, where a huge table was set for at least fifty people. There were plates and goblets and huge silver bowls of fruit, but it looked as if it had been untouched for decades. The fruit was shrivelled up, the silver was tarnished black, and everything was covered in a thick layer of dust. Cobwebs laced the corners of the room and hung from the ceiling. Whatever Sir Maxim was, it was clear that dining was not a regular pastime. Pip looked at the table carefully, but although it was one of the strangest things he'd ever seen, it wasn't going to be any help to him.

He left the room and tried the next door instead, which led into the library. It looked a little more promising – Pip's eye was drawn to a big mahogany desk that was heaped high with papers and journals. He began to look through the drawers, flicking through the documents and notebooks that were stacked up inside. Most of them were to do with the gallery, but Pip kept on searching, wishing that he had a better idea of what he was looking for.

"Pip!" cried Fliss's voice, from the drawing room. At once, Pip dropped the papers and hurried back, wondering if she'd found something. But as he crossed the study, a figure appeared in the doorway. It was Sir Maxim, and he was looking furious.

There was a long, horrible pause, as Sir Maxim stared at the disturbed papers on his desk. Pip grabbed hold of his amulet and held it tightly in his clenched fist.

Sir Maxim stepped forwards and Pip made a desperate run for it, hoping he'd somehow be able to escape, but Sir Maxim seized his arm as he dashed past, forcing him to stop. His grip was incredibly strong, as if his long fingers were made of iron. Pip could feel them pressing into his upper arm.

"Let me go!" he yelled, but Sir Maxim pulled him along, back to the drawing room. He unlocked it and dragged Pip inside. There was Fliss, sitting at a table clutching Splodge. She didn't get up when he entered and although there was no sign of her being restrained, she seemed to be glued to her chair.

"Sit," said Sir Maxim, gesturing to the other empty seat.

Pip shook his head and took out his amulet, brandishing it at Sir Maxim, trying to twist away from him.

"Let me go," he yelled. "Or else."

He had no idea what he thought would happen. There was a part of him that hoped Sir Maxim might reel back at the sight of the amulet, or that the little disc of metal might emit some sort of force that would send him flying. Instead, Sir Maxim simply stared at the amulet, a slight curl of amusement playing on his lips.

"Sit down," he repeated, and Pip, realizing that he had no other option, lowered himself into the chair next to Fliss.

"Why were you going through my things?" asked Sir Maxim, coldly.

Pip and Fliss sat stubbornly silent.

"I warned you before not to pry," he said, and looked at Fliss. "You have no interest in art, do you?"

"I do," she retorted. "Just not the old kind."

"I blame myself for inviting you here," he said. "But I won't make the same mistake again."

"Let us go!" cried Fliss, struggling to get out of her chair. Pip wondered what was holding her there, but when he tried to get to his feet, he found that he couldn't. He was stuck to the seat by some invisible force.

"What have you done?" he yelled, trying to free himself.

"Those are a very rare pair of stickleback chairs," said Sir Maxim. "Once you sit on them, only the owner can let you rise again."

"You can't touch us," said Fliss. "Pip's got an amulet and I've got Splodge."

"Your friend is not in possession of an amulet," said Sir Maxim. "It's simply a useless scrap of metal, something a tourist would buy. I expect you got it from Penelope Crowley. It's the sort of thing she would sell."

He broke off and looked at Splodge.

"The dog, admittedly, is an obstacle," he said. "But as it's currently glued to the chair, I'm not too concerned."

"We're not thirteen," said Pip. "You can't take our spirits. Just fix my parents and we'll leave you alone."

Sir Maxim raised his eyebrows.

"Is that why you've been following me?" he asked. "In that case, you've made a rather serious mistake. I'm not a spirit snatcher."

"You're not?" said Fliss, surprised.

"No," he said. "It's much worse for you than that."

He bared his teeth at them, revealing a pair of long, sharp fangs.

"I'm a vampire."

Sir Maxim advanced upon them, his face gaunt and terrifying in the lamplight.

"Don't!" cried Fliss. "We live here, we're from the alley. There's a code, isn't there, that we leave each other alone?"

"Perhaps you should have remembered that before you broke in here," snarled Sir Maxim. "You seem determined to invade my privacy, so I think it's time for me to put a stop to you."

He bared his teeth again. His long fangs stood out against his thin lips, which were drawn back to reveal his pale gums. The vampire's eyes looked redder than ever as he moved closer, the black pupils fixed firmly upon them. Splodge was growling, but the terrier stayed where he was on Fliss's lap, bound by the same force that kept them stuck to their seats. Pip shrank away from the vampire as he drew near and placed a chilly hand upon Pip's shoulder, the nails biting through his coat and into his flesh.

"We're sorry for coming in here," said Pip, fear making him speak very quickly. "We were just trying to stop the spirit snatcher. It's even attacked Mr Bletchley. We'd have never followed you if we'd known you were a vampire."

"Bletchley has been spirit-snatched?" said Sir Maxim. He loosened his hold on Pip and stared at him. "But he's a ghost."

"Yes," Fliss joined in swiftly. "It only happened yesterday."

"I liked Bletchley," said Sir Maxim, as his fangs receded and his mouth relaxed into a thoughtful expression. "I knew him decades ago, back when he was alive. I assume he's all but vanished now?"

Pip and Fliss nodded.

"Of course, I suspected there might be a spirit snatcher living somewhere in Elbow Alley, ever since I arrived. If I knew who it was, I would certainly have some questions to ask."

He paced around the table and Pip twisted around in his seat, trying to keep an eye on the vampire. But Sir Maxim appeared to have lost his appetite for biting them, at least for the time being.

"I don't like what's happened to Bletchley," said Sir Maxim. "Humans are one thing, of course, but to attack an insider is something else entirely."

"Can you help us find out who it is?" asked Pip.

"No," said Sir Maxim. "It's better to mind one's own business. That way lies the greatest chance of survival. I would advise you to do the same."

"I can't," said Pip bitterly. "It's got my parents, and after my birthday on Saturday, it's going to get me. I don't have a choice."

Sir Maxim sighed.

"You made a great mistake coming here," he said. "Humans aren't safe in a place like Elbow Alley."

"I can't leave," said Pip desperately, wishing that Sir Maxim would understand. "If there was just some way I could find out who the spirit snatcher is, maybe I could persuade it to leave me alone and fix my parents."

Sir Maxim raised his eyebrows.

"I think you are being a little too optimistic," he said. "After all, you have nothing to offer it and everything to lose. I suspect you might find yourselves in even more trouble."

"We've got to try though," said Fliss. "Pip can't just do nothing, can he?"

"I suppose not," said Sir Maxim, who was still looking thoughtful. "I do know someone who is almost certainly a spirit snatcher – she's a little less discreet than the rest of her kind, though just as dangerous. She lives in a different part of London, in one of the other magical enclaves. She is not the sort of acquaintance I care for, but I could see if she's willing to speak with you. I suspect she will let something slip – she usually does. You could find out who the spirit snatcher in Elbow Alley is – and why it attacked Bletchley."

"Does this mean you're letting us go?" said Fliss.

"I am," said Sir Maxim. "I already have several willing donors lined up for my evening feast, and I don't think you'd be as enjoyable a meal."

"We're probably disgusting," agreed Fliss. "I have quite an unhealthy diet."

Sir Maxim clapped his hands together sharply and Pip felt the force that held him to the chair vanish.

He leaped to his feet and Fliss did the same.

"I'll send word if my acquaintance is willing to speak with you," he said. "In the meantime, I hope that I won't ever find you following me again. Next time, I will not be so generous."

Pip and Fliss nodded, and Sir Maxim held the door open for them.

"Now, please, get out of my house."

11

A Ghoulish Encounter

"Well that didn't exactly go as planned," said Pip, as they went back down Elbow Alley.

"No," said Fliss. "And you know what the worst part is? We'll have to meet the ghouls after all. Now that we know our theory about Sir Maxim was wrong, we've got no choice. And they really might tell us who the spirit snatcher is. They seem creepy enough to know that sort of thing."

Pip felt his heart sink. He pulled out his phone and saw that it was almost midnight.

"We'll have to go straight there," he said. "Do you know where this church is? St Whatsitsname's?"

"Course I do," said Fliss. "Follow me."

She turned left down the alley, past Pip's flat and out onto the road beyond, Pip and Splodge following closely behind her.

As it was so late, there weren't many people about, but Pip recognized the familiar hunched figure of Julius up ahead, walking away from them. His hands were deep in the pockets of his long black coat, and his head was down, as if he was studying the pavement.

"Where do you think he's going?" asked Pip, nudging Fliss.

"Nowhere interesting, by the look of him," she said, in a deeply disapproving voice. "Let's cross over – I don't want him to see us."

Fliss had a particularly unnerving style of crossing roads – she didn't bother waiting for a set of lights, but just dashed across as soon as there was a gap in the traffic, pulling an alarmed-looking Splodge along after her. Pip knew exactly how the terrier felt.

Fliss darted down a side street, which led them into a wide empty road.

"This is Dullmarsh Street," she said. "Look, the church is just down there, at the end."

Pip thought he'd never seen such a depressing place – or such an ugly church. It was an austere stone box with an ugly gothic spire stuck on top of it, as if it had been added on as an afterthought. It rose high into the air, dwarfing the surrounding office buildings, which were shut up and dark. St Sepulchre's was encircled by an old graveyard, which had been turned into a windswept courtyard full of benches – the weathered, cracked gravestones were arranged around the edges like rows of giant broken teeth. A stray crisp packet blew across the paving stones and a black council bin was overflowing with sandwich boxes and takeaway wrappers. Pip couldn't understand why anyone would want to sit in such a bleak spot.

"I still don't know why we couldn't have just met them in their shop," said Fliss.

"Maybe the spirit snatcher's got something to do with the church?" suggested Pip.

"Or more likely it's their idea of a fun night out," said Fliss. "Who needs to meet in a restaurant when you've got a graveyard?"

"Where are they?" muttered Pip, looking around for the ghouls. The main door to the church was locked, and there was no sign of Seymour and Deathly outside. High above them, the hands of the church clock were pointing straight upwards. It was midnight. Fliss stepped back into the street to look out for them, dragging a reluctant Splodge along on his lead. The terrier seemed deeply unhappy to still be awake at this hour, and was being as difficult as possible, sitting down at every opportunity and digging his claws into the ground. Pip could hear Fliss coaxing the dog along. He strolled away from them along the side of the church, looking at the line of graves. There was another smaller church door up ahead, and this one was slightly ajar.

"Fliss," he called softly, and beckoned to her to come over.

He pushed the door and it creaked open. Inside, a few candles had been lit, and they cast huge flickering shadows across the soaring stone walls and the high pulpit. The stained-glass windows were dark, and behind the altar was a big wooden crucifix with MEMENTO MORI emblazoned across it. Pip walked across the echoing church and paused before the altar, looking up at the words on the cross.

"It means 'remember you will die'," breathed a damp voice in Pip's ear. "Lovely, isn't it?"

Pip whirled around, his heart racing, and looked into Deathly's pallid face, which was alight with a sort of joyous melancholy.

"Er, hi, Deathly," said Pip.

She gave an angry hiss as Fliss came up to them, still dragging Splodge.

"He's just not happy," said Fliss to Pip, looking worried. "I don't know what's got into him."

Deathly cleared her throat, clearly feeling that Fliss wasn't paying her enough attention.

"Hello," said Fliss. "Where's Seymour?"

"Down there," said Deathly, pointing to a corner, where a set of stone steps led down to the crypt. They were cordoned off by a rope with a sign saying *Private* on it.

"Right," said Fliss, looking at the hole and wrinkling her nose. "Any chance he could come up and we can have our chat here?"

Deathly shook her head violently.

"We go down there," she repeated.

"Okay," said Pip, heading towards it. He was sick of Deathly's creepy behaviour. At that moment, he just wanted to get the meeting over and done with. "If you say so."

He unhooked the rope and they stepped down into the darkness of the crypt. It was very dry and musty, and the cold seeped through his skin, chilling him to the bone. At the bottom of the steps was a narrow paved passageway, lined on either side with shelves, each one stacked with coffins. Some of the coffins were made of

131

wood, others from lead, and a few of the grander ones were carved out of stone. Deathly was lagging behind them. There was no sign of Seymour. Pip and Fliss carried on down the row until they reached a brick wall.

"Where are we going?" said Fliss, turning around. "Oh look, there's Seymour."

Seymour had appeared beside Deathly. The two ghouls were standing side by side across the narrow passageway several metres away from them, and they were grinning strangely.

"He doesn't look any fatter," Deathly whispered to Seymour. "Did you eat your hedgehog?" she said to Pip.

"Doesn't matter," said Seymour, gazing at Pip and Fliss as if he was trying to guess their weight. "They're still much better than the woodlice."

"What did you want to tell us?" asked Pip, although he was beginning to feel deeply uncomfortable. Splodge started to growl softly, a low rumbling noise.

The ghouls began to laugh in a wheezy, mirthless way, a bit like how an accordion would sound if you didn't know how to play it.

"Hee hee," went Seymour. "Hee hee. They believed us."

"We didn't have anything to tell you," croaked Deathly,

looking delighted with herself. "Nothing at all. We don't care a rat's molar about spirit snatchers. We brought you down here to kill you."

"And eat you," added Seymour, licking his pale lips. "Only after a few days though – we'll leave you to get nice and maggoty first."

"No one ever comes down here," said Deathly. "Only us. You'll be safe down here."

Pip looked wildly about him, looking for a way to escape.

"There isn't one," said Deathly, as if she had read his thoughts. "You'll have to go past us, and the thing about ghouls is that we're very good at strangling."

They both started to crack their bony white knuckles and the sound echoed throughout the crypt. Splodge's growls grew louder, and his hackles were up now, his wiry hair standing on end and his teeth bared.

"This is not happening," said Fliss. It was the first time she'd spoken since the ghouls had turned on them, and Pip realized that she was not scared, but absolutely furious. "I'm not going to be strangled by some stupid ghouls. I'm not a *pigeon*, you idiots."

She shouted this last bit and stamped her foot.

Seymour and Deathly screamed at them in fury and

launched themselves forwards, their hands outstretched. Pip got ready to hurl himself at Seymour, who was heading straight for him with a hungry look in his eyes. Deathly, meanwhile, was advancing towards Fliss.

But before either of the ghouls could reach them, a miracle happened. Splodge, who up until this point had been about as aggressive as a stuffed toy, flew at the ghouls, his lead whirling in the air behind him, a spitting, snarling whirlwind of rage. He leaped up at them, and sank his teeth deep into Seymour's leg. The ghoul screeched and flung the dog off, but the attack had unbalanced him. He fell backwards, crashing into one of the shelves. The wood must have been rotten because it snapped like matchsticks. A stack of coffins tumbled down. They were the heavy old-fashioned kind, made from lead and stone. Seymour was buried beneath them, while Deathly howled as a particularly ornate marble coffin landed on her foot.

Splodge had somehow avoided the landslide completely. He trotted towards them, completely unharmed and looking extremely pleased with himself.

"Good boy!" cried Fliss, kneeling down beside him. "You clever, clever dog."

Pip crouched down and patted Splodge too, ruffling

his sandy fur, while Deathly shrieked and Seymour moaned.

"Let's get out of here," said Pip, straightening up at last. They climbed over the mass of coffins and broken shelves, taking care to give the trapped ghouls a wide berth.

"Help us," said Deathly, as they slipped past. "We didn't mean to—"

"You're pathetic," said Fliss, cutting her off. "Try that again and I swear you won't survive it."

They hurried towards the stairs, glancing back every few steps to make sure the ghouls hadn't got free. But they were stuck. Seymour had managed to wiggle one arm through a gap in the rubble and was waving it about limply, while Deathly was switching between trying to tug her own leg free and trying to push the coffins off her husband.

"Isn't it a bit cruel to leave them both in here?" said Pip, hesitating at the top of the stairs. Much as he was revolted by the ghouls, it still seemed wrong to leave them.

"They'll just have another go at killing us if we free them," said Fliss matter-of-factly. "The lying, rotten creeps."

"I know, but what if Seymour dies under there?"

"Ghouls can't die – worse luck," said Fliss. "They're just going to have to stay down here until someone manages to shift all that rubble. Personally, I hope no one comes into this crypt for a very long time."

They emerged back into the church, and the air seemed warm compared to the ice-cold crypt. They replaced the rope, ignoring the faint wails of Deathly and Seymour, and left the church as fast as they could. Splodge trotted between them, his tail held high.

"I'm going to give you the biggest meal as soon as we get home," Fliss told him. "Chicken, steak, whatever you like."

Splodge wagged his tail happily and the three of them headed back to Elbow Alley. They were no closer to finding the spirit snatcher, but at least they were still alive.

12

The Halloween House

Pip overslept the next morning and was awoken by the sound of someone violently hammering at the front door. Thinking it might be Fliss, he quickly got dressed and went downstairs to open it, only to find a furious Penny puffed up in the doorway.

"You!" she shrieked. "Let me in – I want a word with your parents."

Pip tried to close the door quickly but she pushed it open so that he was squashed against the wall. She charged past him, up the stairs and into the sitting room, where his parents were slumped in their usual spots.

"Your son is a monster!" she screamed at them. "Stealing from me! Playing nasty practical jokes! You should be ashamed of him!"

His mother and father just watched her as if she was

one of their television programmes.

Penny continued to rant at them until she realized that she was getting no response whatsoever.

"What's the matter with them?" she snapped, turning to Pip.

"They've been spirit-snatched," he replied flatly.

"Oh," she said, looking shocked. "That's still no excuse for your behaviour."

"No," agreed Pip. He fumbled in his pocket for the little silver disc.

"Here's the amulet," he said, giving it back to her. "I'm sorry for taking it."

She grabbed it and glared at him.

"And I'm sorry about the vase. It was an accident, honestly. I'll work in the shop for as long as you like, to make up for it."

"I never want you in my shop again," she said. "Never. After that nasty practical joke you pulled...I haven't been able to sit down since."

"That was an accident too," said Pip. "I just put it on the chair without thinking, then forgot about it. I'd never do something like that on purpose, I promise."

But Penny was too ruffled and upset to listen. She seemed to swell with rage, and her claws made a nasty scratching sound on the carpet. Pip stepped back, in case she was about to strike at him.

"You should watch out, Pip Ruskin," she said. "Outsiders like you never last for long."

With that, she turned, her pink coat whirling about her, and stomped away. Her talons made it difficult for her to go down the stairs, so she had to turn sideways, glaring all the while, and she slammed the door so hard she nearly broke the hinges. The sound reverberated angrily around the flat.

Pip sighed and sat down on the sofa, in between his parents. A stack of unpaid bills was piling up on the rickety side table and the room was still full of cardboard boxes that no one had bothered to unpack. Pip suddenly felt very alone. A wave of despair welled up inside him. What if he was never able to fix his parents? And what if he had his spirit snatched too – what would happen to them all then? His birthday was tomorrow and time was running out.

"Please talk to me," he begged, looking from his mother to his father. "You must be in there somewhere."

They just stared dully back at him as if they didn't know who he was. It was the worst feeling in the world, having his parents look at him like that.

"I used to wish you were boring," he said out loud. "I hated how different you were compared to everyone else. But now I'd give anything if you'd go back to how you were. It wasn't so bad, after all. I just didn't realize."

It was as if he'd spoken to the wall. They just sat there in silence, surrounded by the sea of bills, until someone started hammering on the door again.

This time, Pip inched it open suspiciously, wondering if it was Penny again.

"What's the matter?" Fliss stood on the doorstep, accompanied as usual by Splodge.

"Thank goodness it's you," said Pip, and opened the door.

"I heard yelling," said Fliss. "What happened?"

"Penny came over. She wasn't happy."

"I'm sure she'll simmer down eventually," said Fliss, and gave a sudden snort of laughter. "Sorry, it's just every time I think of her sitting on that hedgehog…"

"Hilarious," said Pip, feeling that it was a lot less funny if you were the one being blamed for it.

"Anyway, that's not why I came round. Sir Maxim sent over a note."

She stepped out of the street and into the hall, and thrust a neatly folded sheet of paper at Pip. He read it at once.

Dear Felicity,

I have contacted Myra Qwirm and she is willing to meet you and your friend this afternoon at three. Her address is 19 Turnabout Crescent, N1 2ZZ. I have not told her why you are calling, and you must be <u>extremely</u> careful what you say. Do not, under any circumstances, confront her directly about spirit snatchers – it will not end well. You are taking an extraordinary risk in pursuing this course of action, but I wish you luck.

Kind regards,

Maximilian Vane

"Let's make a plan this time," he said, handing the note back to Fliss.

"We already have a plan! Find out any information about the spirit snatcher, then work out the best way of stopping it. Simple."

"I mean, let's have a strategy for getting out of there alive," Pip elaborated.

"We'll take Splodge," said Fliss, glancing down at the terrier. "Mr Whipple was right that he's good for protection – he's already proved he's way better than that stupid amulet."

"It wasn't a real amulet, remember?"

"Whatever," said Fliss. "You can't deny Splodge is useful."

"He is," said Pip. "But I think we should be more careful. We're going to meet a spirit snatcher – she could be even more dangerous than the ghouls."

"She won't go for us. We're still underage – just. And anyway, since I'm only half-human I'm probably safe anyway. Well, safer than you."

"I know," said Pip, not even bothering to question her this time. "You've only mentioned it about a million times. I just meant do you think we should split up? One of us goes in and talks to her, and the other one waits outside? That way if whoever's in there gets into trouble, the other one can get help."

"Definitely not," said Fliss. "If she does try anything, it's better that we're together. It'll be fine. Let's just act pleasant, butter her up, and get her to spill the beans."

"You're being way too relaxed about it," said Pip. "Anything could happen. It makes more sense if we split up. I'll go in and speak to her, you can stay outside."

"I don't care what the sensible thing to do is," cried Fliss. "I want us to go in there together."

"Fliss—" Pip tried again, but she cut him off and he realized that for the first time since he had known her, she was looking upset.

"I don't want either of us to get hurt," she said. "We're

friends, aren't we? And friends should stick together."

Pip was so astonished that he simply stared at her. No one had ever said that he was their friend before, not properly.

"What?" said Fliss defensively. "Why are you looking at me like that?"

"Nothing," said Pip. "You're right. Let's both go and speak to her."

Several hours later, they took the Tube across London. Pip had never been on the Underground before, and found the rattling carriages, the stifling tunnels and the endless escalators exhausting. He was grateful that Fliss, at least, was used to it and led the way to the right platform. They crammed themselves onto the Central Line, which was so packed they couldn't even find a place to stand without being crushed by about six people at once. Pip fought to find a handhold on a rail that had at least eight other commuters clinging to it, while Fliss had to clutch Splodge to her chest so that he didn't get squashed on the floor of the carriage.

They tumbled out at Tottenham Court Road and changed to the Northern Line, which was equally rattly but thankfully a lot quieter. They flopped down onto a pair of empty seats with relief, and Fliss set Splodge down on the floor between them.

"Four stops to go," she said, her eyes on one of the maps that were pasted along the top of the carriage, beside adverts for food deliveries and dating sites. Pip looked at the young woman sitting opposite. She was only a few years older than they were and very noticeable with her cropped blue hair, bright blue eyes and shiny black leather coat. However, by far the oddest thing about her was the fact that she was shuffling a deck of tarot cards, and turning them over, one by one.

Pip elbowed Fliss in the ribs.

"D'you think she's...you know...one of you lot?"

Fliss cast an appraising glance at the blue-haired girl.

"Possibly," she said.

Pip had a feeling that the girl had overheard him, although she kept her eyes cast downwards on her cards.

The train lurched to a stop and the girl got up.

As she passed them, she waved a card at Pip.

"Ten of swords," she said. "You should be careful. And so should you," she added, glancing at Fliss.

"What do you mean?" asked Pip, but the girl had

already stepped out onto the platform and the doors swooshed shut behind her.

"Don't take it too seriously," advised Fliss. "It probably meant nothing. You get all sorts in London."

But Pip couldn't help wondering if the cards knew something they didn't.

They eventually emerged into a different part of London. It was different to the area surrounding Elbow Alley – busier, the sort of place where people lived as well as worked. Pip had become so used to the alley's rhythms – the quiet residents and the faceless throng of office workers – that he'd forgotten what a normal lived-in street looked like. Babies were being pushed along in prams, elderly women were carrying bags of shopping, and people in exercise gear jogged along the pavements. Pip began to wonder whether they'd got the address wrong. It didn't seem possible that a community of magical beings could exist in this bustling corner of the city.

"Do you know where we're going?" Pip asked Fliss, and she frowned.

"I'm not the one with the fancy phone, am I?" she said, and Pip knew that she was annoyed at having to admit that her own mobile phone looked and functioned like a brick. Fliss frequently bemoaned her mother's strong views on excessive internet usage.

"I'll check," he said, and searched for directions to Turnabout Crescent. The little arrow guided them first down one street, and then another, as they turned away from the high street, up a hill and down past several blocks of red-brick council flats. It led them into Turnabout Square and there the directions stopped.

"You must have typed it in wrong," said Fliss, peering over Pip's shoulder.

"I didn't," he said. "It said it was here. Anyway, if this is Turnabout Square we must be close."

They did an entire circuit of the square, past faceless grey house after faceless grey house until they arrived back at the same spot, their tempers slightly frayed. Splodge sat down and refused to budge, just gazed into the distance with an annoyingly vacant expression.

"I'm not picking you up," Fliss told him. "I've carried you enough for today. You're getting lazy."

Pip followed the dog's gaze, which was directed at a corner of the square, and noticed something they had both missed.

"Look!" he cried, pointing. "Between those two houses on the corner. There's another street – it's hidden behind that tree."

Fliss bounded forwards and so did Splodge.

"You're right," she cried. "There's a sign too – it's Turnabout Crescent."

The street curved away from the square, into a semicircle with a private garden in the middle of it. The garden's iron gates were locked, and an official-looking sign read *No Mobile Phones. No Children. No Outsiders.* The surrounding crescent of large terraced villas were all painted white, with columns on either side of the front doors. Every single house was covered with the most incredible Halloween decorations Pip had ever seen. Entire cartloads of pumpkins were heaped on their stone steps, and the windows were decorated with vast cobwebs, gigantic spiders and groups of grinning skeletons. *A WITCH LIVES HERE!* read one huge hand-painted sign, while another said *TRICKS ONLY, NO TREATS.* Some houses had special effects, so the sounds of screams and groans and evil cackles wafted gently across the air, while another one was completely covered in hundreds of broomsticks, making it look as if someone had tried to thatch it but had done the walls by mistake.

"Wow," said Pip, as they surveyed the scene. "Does everyone magical take Halloween this seriously?"

"Not in the alley," said Fliss, who seemed as bowled

over as Pip was. "There's our party in the pub, and a few of the shopkeepers decorate a bit, but nothing like this."

Number nineteen was easy to spot, because it was the one with the most decorations. There were pumpkins and lanterns all along the railings outside, life-size plastic witches and vampires and zombies were attached to the roof, and the entire outside of it had been painted in black and orange stripes.

They went up the steps to the front door, past large buckets of brightly coloured sweets.

"How come no one's eaten them?" said Fliss, picking one up and unwrapping it. A stone fell into her palm.

"That explains it," she muttered and dropped it back into the nearest bucket.

Pip reached for the door knocker, which had been replaced by a severed rubber hand. It let out a loud scream when he touched it and Pip leaped back. He could hear the scream echoing around the inside of the house.

A moment later, a woman answered the door. She was squat and square and her large mouth was slicked with orange lipstick, which matched the front of her house but didn't suit her in the slightest. Her colourless hair was cut short, and she wore a grey trouser suit. This woman certainly didn't look like Pip's idea of a spirit snatcher, or, in fact, like any sort of magical being at all. She looked as if she'd spent her life doing an incredibly dull office job.

She frowned when she saw Fliss and Pip standing on the doorstep.

"Mrs Qwirm?" asked Pip.

"Miss," she said, still looking annoyed. "Dear Sir Maxim told me you were keen to speak with me, but he didn't tell me how very young you both are. Why, you're *children*."

She narrowed her eyes and stared at them both.

"How old are you?" she asked. "Seven? Eight?"

"No," retorted Fliss. "We're thirteen tomorrow, actually."

"Tomorrow?" repeated Miss Qwirm, sounding interested. Pip elbowed Fliss sharply.

"We're still twelve," he said quickly. "I hope it's all right, us being younger."

"We don't really encourage children around here," she replied. "We're all very grown up in Turnabout Crescent."

Given the ridiculous amount of Halloween decorations adorning the houses, this seemed to Pip like a very strange thing to say.

"But you can come in," she said at last, and stood aside to let them pass. "Since you're so nearly old enough." Then her eyes fell on Splodge and her face changed.

"Oh dear," she said. "No, this will never do."

"What?" asked Fliss.

"The dog. No, dear, this is simply not going to work. I can't have a dirty animal leaving muddy pawprints all over my lovely clean house. Can't you leave her somewhere?"

"Him," said Fliss. "And no, I can't. Splodge goes wherever I go."

"Very well," said Miss Qwirm, but her lips were pressed tightly together, smearing the hideous orange lipstick. "Wait here a moment."

She left them on the doormat and disappeared inside. A minute later, she returned, brandishing a large wodge of newspaper.

"You can come inside now," she said. "But you must be careful to only step on the paper."

They went inside and saw that she had laid a trail of newspaper sheets all the way down her white tiled hallway, which was lined with cardboard cut-outs of yet more pumpkins. Fliss went first, going from sheet to sheet like they were stepping stones, clutching an unhappy

Splodge in her arms. They proceeded in single file, with Miss Qwirm a little way in front, laying down more newspaper as she went.

"We're just going in here," she said, backing into a large drawing room. Everything was a pale beige – the walls, the furniture and the thick carpet that covered the floor. There were no paintings on the walls, just a pair of large rectangular mirrors, each of them framed by a pair of beige satin curtains. Miss Qwirm guided them, sheet by sheet, to one of the sofas and they sat down gingerly. Fliss stuck Splodge on her lap and tried very hard to make sure none of his paws were spilling over onto the upholstery. Miss Qwirm's eyes were on the dog too, and she didn't look pleased.

"I thought we'd have some refreshments," she said finally. "Melody! Melody!"

A dead-eyed maid appeared, dressed in a beige uniform and pushing a gigantic trolley that was heaving with cakes, drinks bottles, and a great deal of crockery.

"I was going to suggest cocktails to start with, but as you're children, Melody can mix you up some mocktails instead." She had a particularly irritating way of saying "children", as if the word was in inverted commas. Pip tried to let it wash over him. Fliss didn't seem to notice.

She was too busy wrestling with Splodge, who seemed determined to wipe himself on the sofa cushions.

Miss Qwirm beckoned the maid over and whispered something in her ear. Melody nodded, then began to pour a stream of bright-red cherry syrup into two cocktail glasses, added a dash of something from a little glass bottle, then started fiddling around with twists of lemon peel and dashes of orangeade.

"So why are you here to see me?" asked Miss Qwirm, as she settled back in her beige armchair. "Dear Sir Maxim didn't say."

"Something's happened to my parents and he thought you might be able to help," said Pip.

"They've been spirit-snatched," put in Fliss.

"Spirit-snatched?" Miss Qwirm frowned. "What's that got to do with me?"

"I'm not sure," said Pip awkwardly. "It's just that he said you were the best person to talk to."

"And why did he say that?" said Miss Qwirm. Although her mouth had arranged itself into a smile, her eyes were unfriendly. Pip didn't know how to reply. He remembered Sir Maxim's warning and resolved not to annoy her if he could possibly help it.

His gaze fell upon the mirrors again and he wondered

why anyone would bother to put curtains around them. It seemed like an odd thing to do. Miss Qwirm caught him staring and frowned. Pip looked away quickly.

Melody came over with a pair of mocktails on a beige tray. She held it out to Fliss and Pip and they each took one. Splodge sniffed at Fliss's drink and butted it with his head, almost knocking it out of her hand.

"Careful!" cried Miss Qwirm.

"Sorry," muttered Fliss, struggling to restrain Splodge.

"Drink up!" said Miss Qwirm, clapping her hands together.

Pip took a small sip and instantly regretted it. The drink was sickly sweet, undercut with a faint taste of something bitter. Miss Qwirm gave him an encouraging, if slightly unnerving smile. Then she turned to Melody, who was standing next to her armchair, gazing vacantly into space.

"Just a gin and tonic for me," she said, and watched the maid as she started fiddling around with yet more lemon peel. Fliss quickly leaned towards Pip.

"Don't touch the drink," she hissed. "She's put something in it – I can smell it's not right. Get rid of it."

With a smooth motion, Fliss tipped her glass so that it spilled down behind the back of the sofa, then immediately turned her attention back to Splodge. When Miss Qwirm looked around a moment later, Fliss was looking innocent, with an empty glass in her hand.

"Delicious, isn't it?" said Miss Qwirm, with an approving nod at Fliss. She looked pointedly at Pip, who raised his still-full glass to his mouth again. This time, he made sure to keep his lips pressed tightly together. He wished there was some way he could get rid of it without her noticing.

"I know spirit snatchers choose to stay hidden," he tried again. "But isn't there anything you could tell us about them?"

"Have another sip of that drink first," she said. "Then I'll explain exactly what's happened to your parents."

She leaned forwards, staring at him expectantly, the fake smile still plastered to her face. Out of the corner of his eye, Pip saw Fliss shaking her head, willing him not to do it.

"You'll tell me?" he asked.

"I promise," said Miss Qwirm.

Pip took a gulp of the drink. It was horrible, for all its sweetness, and sloshed thickly around his mouth like cough medicine. In its own way, it was as bad as a fermented Brussels sprout. He pretended to swallow, but didn't.

"Good," said Miss Qwirm, with a satisfied expression. Fliss looked horrified.

"Spirit snatchers occupy the most important position in the magical community," Miss Qwirm began, sounding a bit like a bossy schoolteacher. "If it wasn't for them, how would a poor defenceless hag or a simple ghoul ever survive undetected amongst the humans?"

"But they spirit—" began Fliss, but Miss Qwirm cut her off with a cough.

"I prefer to use the term 'calming'," she said. "Certain humans can get a little too inquisitive, a little too excitable, and spirit snatchers simply remove those troublesome excess spirits. And once a spirit snatcher has done its work, there's simply no undoing it. Not unless they are destroyed, of course."

She broke off, and gave a little shudder.

"As for your parents, dear, they must have needed it. It's only the overly excitable ones who are calmed in the first place. Most people are so balanced that there's no excess spirits for a spirit snatcher to feed off."

Pip felt sick, and not just because of the disgusting drink that was sloshing around his mouth.

"Take dear Melody," she continued, gesturing to the maid. "She used to be quite beside herself, poor thing.

Rushing about, not knowing if she was coming or going, getting troubled by all manner of meddlesome thoughts. Look at her now. Isn't she so much better?"

Melody gave Miss Qwirm a ghost of a smile. She had that same defeated look that Pip's father had as he sat slumped on the sofa, the look of someone who was simply existing, waiting for life to go by. Miss Qwirm looked at Pip, who gazed silently back at her. He knew he couldn't keep up the pretence much longer – he wished she would turn away, so that he could spit out the drink. He was beginning to feel slightly dizzy.

"Your parents will improve a little, over time," continued Miss Qwirm. "They'll talk more, they'll even be able to get jobs, like Melody has. It just takes a while for the recently calmed to settle into their new personalities. You'll experience that for yourself, before too long."

Pip's headache was getting worse. He wished he'd never come. It took all of his self-control not to spit out the sickening cherry mocktail. He clenched his jaw and closed his eyes.

"You've gone very quiet," said Miss Qwirm, sounding more pleased than concerned. "Getting tired, dear? I'm not surprised."

Pip nodded, still unable to say a word.

"Of course, even though spirit snatchers are the most powerful of magical beings, we still need to protect ourselves from those who would do us harm," she continued, helping herself to an iced pink cupcake from the trolley. "Assuming our vaporous form exposes us to danger – it's why we take such care to conceal ourselves. By staying hidden, we can control the magical communities while we feed on human spirits. We choose to spare our fellow magical beings, but we're perfectly capable of calming them if they become a little too troublesome. If we keep to the shadows, everyone fears us."

She said these last words with relish, as she bit into her cupcake.

"Could you tell us who the spirit snatcher in Elbow Alley is?" asked Fliss. "Or pass on a message?"

Miss Qwirm put down her cake and frowned.

"Melody, I think our little friend could do with another of the special mocktails," she said. "She's far too lively."

"I don't want another…" began Fliss.

"I insist," said Miss Qwirm.

"And you need to finish your drink too," she said, nodding at Pip's glass. "After everything I've said, I can't have you telling tales."

Pip didn't know what to do. He picked up the drink and held it to his lips, but he couldn't take another sip without swallowing first, and he knew that would be an extremely bad idea.

"Don't!" Fliss lunged forwards and knocked the glass out of Pip's hand. It rolled around the floor and a bright red stain spread across the beige carpet.

"How dare you!" cried Miss Qwirm, swelling with fury. Pip choked and spat out the rest of his drink, which added to the puddle on the carpet. Splodge leaped off Fliss's lap and crashed into the drinks trolley, sending china and cakes flying in all directions. Miss Qwirm lunged for Pip's wrist, but he ducked away.

"Neither of you are leaving this house until you're old enough to be calmed!" she yelled. "Melody! Lock the door!"

"Quick!" yelled Fliss, and she sprinted for the exit, Pip and Splodge close behind. Melody hadn't reacted as quickly as they had – she seemed to be in a daze – and they shot past her, into the hall.

"You wait until my friend in Elbow Alley hears about this!" screamed Miss Qwirm. "You won't remember your own names when they've finished with you!"

Pip and Fliss raced through the front door and

slammed it shut behind them, so that the severed-hand door knocker swung wildly. They sped down the steps to the street, not stopping until they were a safe distance from the house.

"She was trying to drug us…" panted Fliss. "Knock us out until she was able to spirit-snatch us. Imagine if we'd drunk it."

"Yeah," agreed Pip, trying to catch his breath. Now he was out in the fresh air, his headache was beginning to fade. "How did you guess she'd put something in the drinks?"

"It smelt weird," replied Fliss. "Also, Splodge was acting funny – I could tell something was up. I can't believe Sir Maxim thought it was a good idea for us to meet her – maybe he was hoping she'd finish us off. She didn't reveal *anything* about the spirit snatcher in Elbow Alley."

"But she did say something important," said Pip. "Once someone's been attacked, they'll stay like that unless the spirit snatcher who did it is destroyed. We can't persuade the spirit snatcher in Elbow Alley to fix my parents, because they won't be able to."

"I hadn't thought of that," admitted Fliss.

Pip stared gloomily at a nearby pumpkin. Instead of

getting closer to their goal, it seemed to be moving further out of their reach. All they'd done was to draw more attention to themselves.

"Don't, Pip," said Fliss, in a warning voice.

"What?" he asked.

"Give up. I know what you're thinking, and you can't. You're thirteen tomorrow, remember? You'll be 'calmed' before you know it – I could be too. We need to do something. Should we try again?"

She nodded back towards Miss Qwirm's house.

"There's no point," said Pip. "She'll be on her guard now. Perhaps it won't be so bad, being spirit-snatched. Maybe I'll even be happier."

"How can you say that?" cried Fliss. "Look at your parents! Do you really want to go around like some shell of a person? You should be happy that you're different, that you've got some life in you."

At that moment Melody opened the door of number nineteen, a bin bag in her hand.

"Do you want to end up like that poor girl?" hissed Fliss. "Do you?"

"Of course I don't," Pip retorted. "I'm just saying that our stupid plan isn't working."

"Don't you dare call my plan stupid." Fliss was glaring

at him now. For a moment it seemed as if they were about to have an argument, but Melody started walking towards them, and they realized that they were standing beside a line of wheelie bins. They stopped talking and stared warily at the maid.

"Should we run for it?" said Fliss in a low voice.

"I don't think she'll do anything," said Pip. "She's acting just like my parents."

Sure enough, Melody gave no sign that she recognized them as she drew near. She just put her bag of rubbish in the bin without saying a word.

Then Splodge trotted up to her and gave a little whine, as if he was begging her to notice him. Her vacant face broke into a small smile. Splodge jumped up at her, putting his forepaws on her legs, and she stroked his head, then squatted down and tickled the terrier's ears. He promptly rolled over so that she could rub his stomach. His paws waved in the air and his mouth opened in a toothy grin.

"I like dogs," Melody murmured, more to herself than to Pip or Fliss.

"He's called Splodge," said Fliss.

"Splodge," repeated Melody.

"We're looking for one of Miss Qwirm's friends," said

Pip, feeling that anything was worth a go. "They live in Elbow Alley."

Melody didn't respond. It was as if he hadn't spoken.

"Do you know their name?" tried Pip again.

"Or what they look like?" chipped in Fliss.

Melody still said nothing, and continued to bend over the dog.

"My parents have been spirit-snatched," Pip persisted. "And tomorrow, there's a good chance that Fliss and I will be attacked too. If there's anything you can tell us, anything at all, it might help."

Something flickered across Melody's face, as if a shadow of her former self had floated to the surface for a moment.

"Octavian," she said, in a low voice.

"What was that?" asked Pip, not quite certain if he'd heard her correctly.

"He's called Octavian," she said, in a slightly clearer voice.

"Do you know his surname?" tried Pip. "Or where exactly in Elbow Alley we can find him?"

But Melody's face had turned blank again. She got to her feet and stood looking down at Splodge for a moment.

"He's a nice dog," she said finally. Then she walked off, back towards Miss Qwirm's house, without saying another word.

"That was weird," said Fliss. "But I suppose it's better than nothing. Let's track down this Octavian. At the very least we might be able to persuade them not to attack anyone else. And you never know, there still might be some way of helping your parents."

She set off at a brisk march, past the madly decorated houses, barely even flinching when a robotic skeleton jumped out right in front of them. Pip hurried after her, wondering how she could be so confident when they had so little to work with. A memory of his old life in Norwich rose up in his mind. It was almost laughable that back then his biggest worries had been a smelly lunchbox and a garage full of incontinent birds. It had all been so simple, so safe, and he hadn't even known it.

"Stop looking like that," said Fliss, not slowing her pace.

"Like what?"

"Like Seymour did back in that crypt, when he was being squashed by five coffins at once," she said. "Cheer up. It might be harder than we first thought, but we'll sort that stupid spirit snatcher out, you'll see. Between the two of us, we'll manage it."

She sounded so determined that Pip couldn't help but feel a little better. Even though his life had become so much stranger and more dangerous since he'd moved to London, there was one tremendous improvement. He had a friend, possibly even two, if you counted Splodge. No matter how bad things got, Pip thought, it didn't seem quite so awful if you were friends with someone like Fliss.

13

The Unluckiest Number

Pip and Fliss had planned to start hunting down the mysterious Octavian as soon as they returned to Elbow Alley. However, it was after seven o'clock when they got back, and Fliss's father instantly popped out of the pub cellar like a large jack-in-the-box.

"Where have you been?" he demanded, managing to sound both furious and worried at the same time. "You're late for dinner. I've been beside myself. No one in the alley knew where you were."

"We're fine," said Fliss in a soothing tone.

"I can see that," replied Mr Wells, frowning at his daughter. "But there's a spirit snatcher about and you're almost thirteen. You need to stay inside where I can keep an eye on you."

His gaze travelled to Pip.

"And you should be at home too. It's not safe for you to be roaming about. Keep the doors and windows locked – if the spirit snatcher strikes, it's more likely to be at night."

He ushered Fliss and Splodge into the pub before Fliss had chance to say another word. Pip gazed after them, then made his way home, suddenly feeling exceptionally nervous at what the night ahead might bring.

Back at the flat, he checked the doors and the windows. He even plugged the gaps beneath the doors with towels, remembering how the spirit snatcher had seemed to seep through them on that first night in Elbow Alley. Pip felt as if the best chance of survival was to not go to bed at all, so he sat with his parents until long after midnight, checking the doors and windows every time he heard the faintest clatter or creak. Even though his mother and father were still staring at the television, he found their presence comforting. If he closed his eyes, he could almost imagine that they were still their usual selves. He never imagined that he would miss their peculiar habits so badly. He was still mulling over the strangeness of that thought when, despite himself, he drifted off to sleep.

Pip awoke with a jolt. It was Halloween – the day of his thirteenth birthday. He blinked, looked around him and then was overwhelmed by relief as his brain filled with its familiar jumble of worries and thoughts. By some miracle, he hadn't had his spirit snatched. He prised himself off the sofa and stood up. His limbs felt stiff and sore, yet his parents were still seated in exactly the same position as they had been last night, as if it hadn't even occurred to them to go to bed. He wasn't even sure if they were asleep or not.

He had a feeling that this birthday was going to be very different to his previous ones. His parents were usually very good at spoiling him, even though they didn't have much money. The year before, he had been given a new phone – not the latest model, but a fairly good one – and the year before that, a second-hand bicycle. His mother also baked him a special chocolate fudge birthday cake, even though she normally disapproved of things like sugar and milk chocolate and golden syrup. There was no chance of her baking a cake this year.

"Guess what day it is?" he asked them.

"Um," said Mr Ruskin, who was staring at *The Crazy*

Fun Breakfast Show with his mouth open. Mrs Ruskin appeared not to have heard him.

"It's my birthday today," said Pip. It came out louder than he'd meant it to. At last, his parents looked up at him.

"Happy birthday," said his father.

"Happy Easter," said his mother absent-mindedly.

Usually Pip's birthdays began with pancakes – slightly rubbery buckwheat ones, but pancakes nonetheless – and a breakfast table with several brightly wrapped presents on it. This time, there was nothing, no sign whatsoever that he had turned thirteen. Pip had been expecting this, but he hadn't anticipated how bad it would make him feel. His mouth started to tremble, forming an unhappy downwards curve, and he knew he was moments away from crying.

He was fighting the sensation as hard as he could when someone rapped at the door downstairs. Feeling cautious, he stuck his head out of the sitting-room window and looked down, half expecting to see Penny again. It was Fliss.

"Are you okay?" she called, peering up at him. "Did you survive the night?"

"Yes!" said Pip, feeling immensely pleased to see her. "I'll come down – hang on."

"I'm busy this morning," said Fliss mysteriously. "Dad and I have lots to do. I'll come over later – just before sunset. Happy birthday, by the way."

She gave him a cheerful wave and disappeared.

Pip felt even worse as he shut the window and looked glumly around his flat. He was beginning to feel horribly alone. Fliss clearly had other things to occupy her. She was probably heading back to enjoy a special birthday breakfast of her own. He suddenly felt immensely overwhelmed by his situation too – he had thought that they would have solved the mystery of the spirit snatcher by now, but it felt as if they were no closer than they were at the start. They had a name – assuming that Melody was telling the truth – but that didn't feel like much to go on now that he could have his spirit snatched at any moment.

For the first time he wondered if he really should leave Elbow Alley – at least for a little while. He could go and stay with his grandparents in Scotland. That was far enough away to be safe and he was pretty sure that there wasn't any magical activity happening in his grandparents' quiet suburban street. It would give him more time to figure out how to fix his parents. If he could persuade his parents to come too, then maybe he could find another way of helping them without having to confront the spirit snatcher.

Pip had the landline number of his grandparents saved on his phone – neither of them owned mobiles – and on an impulse, he called it. It rang for ages. He was about to hang up when his grandmother finally answered the phone.

"Hello?" she said. "If you're trying to sell us something, we're not interested."

"It's me – Pip."

"Oh, Pip!" she cried, breathlessly. "What a lovely surprise! We were just leaving the house, we've got a taxi waiting outside. Happy birthday! We wanted to send you a card but we'd no idea how to get hold of you. Your parents seem to have vanished off the face of the earth."

"They're still here," said Pip. "Sort of."

"I'm sure your father's just forgotten about us because he's so busy with his shop – we can't wait to come down and see it," said his grandmother, speaking very quickly. In the background, Pip could hear the sound of a car-horn beeping impatiently.

"Something's happ—" he began, but his grandmother carried on talking.

"I'd love to have a chat but we're just heading off

to the airport. We're going on holiday – three weeks in Majorca. Isn't that wonderful?"

"Wonderful," echoed Pip faintly.

"Have a lovely birthday and we'll see you at Christmas," she said. Pip said goodbye and hung up.

The situation seemed even more hopeless than before. There was no way out after all. He was stuck in Elbow Alley.

Pip didn't leave the flat that day. He told himself it was because he was thinking of how to track down Octavian, but the truth was he was feeling so miserable he seemed to have become rooted to the spot. He wondered if this was what it felt like to have your spirit snatched. It was a relief when Fliss finally reappeared as dusk fell.

She thrust a brightly wrapped package into his hands as soon as he opened the door.

"I got you a present."

Pip tore off the neon-yellow paper and unfolded a dark grey tee shirt that was covered with constellations of silver stars.

"I know you like grey," she said. "But this seemed a bit more like you than those identical grey sweaters…"

She broke off, looking at the sky-blue jumper that

Pip was wearing today. It was another of Mrs Ruskin's handmade creations and Pip had realized that it was actually quite nice. He couldn't understand why he'd never noticed before.

"It's brilliant," he said, admiring the tee shirt and feeling a huge surge of gratitude towards Fliss. "I feel really bad though – I didn't get you anything."

"Don't be stupid," said Fliss. "I've got loads of presents, and I had a feeling your parents wouldn't be able to remember your birthday, so I wanted to make sure you got something. We're friends. That's what friends do."

"Really?" For the first time that day, Pip felt a blaze of happiness well up inside him.

"Really," said Fliss with a grin, and she linked her arm through his. "Come with me – I've got another surprise for you."

She led Pip a few steps down Elbow Alley until they reached The Ragged Hare.

"Go ahead," she said and Pip, mystified, went into the pub.

It had been decked out for a party – hundreds of black balloons were bumping against the ceiling and carved pumpkins were dotted about the tables and windowsills, each one casting a glowing light from their grinning faces. There was a large sign pinned up across the top of the bar, spelling out the words *HAPPY BIRTHDAYS* in large gold letters. Several of the regulars were already installed at the bar and wished them both a happy birthday as soon as they appeared.

"Good, isn't it?" said Fliss, grinning at the surprised look on his face. "Dad and I spent all morning blowing up the balloons – I thought we could have a joint celebration. He and Mum throw me a party in here every year – they invite all the people they know in Elbow Alley and all of our relatives who live nearby. Mum's really upset she had to be away – she's left me about a million presents and rung me about three times already – but it's good you're here instead."

Fliss lowered her voice, so her father couldn't hear. "It would have been the most depressing birthday ever otherwise." Then she continued in a more businesslike tone, "It's also an excellent opportunity to ask around, see if we can find out who Octavian is."

More people were starting to trickle into the pub now. Fliss and her father were clearly popular, because there were a lot of people who Pip had never seen before. They all had the same, slightly wild look, and Pip knew without asking that they belonged to the magical world instead of the human one. Some familiar faces appeared too – Mr Whipple from the bookshop arrived promptly, bearing two enormous boxes of chocolates, and presented one to Fliss and the other to Pip. Mrs Ramirez from the café appeared with an enormous plate of empanadas and a steaming pot of something that smelt delicious, but had an eyeball floating in it. Penny came in, bringing a bunch of flowers for Fliss and a scowl for Pip. It was obvious that she still hadn't forgiven him.

As the light outside faded, more people joined the party. Sir Maxim made an unexpected appearance, accompanied by the pale girl who had been guarding the door to his house at the exhibition opening.

"Happy birthday!" he said, and shook their hands. "I hope your visit to Miss Qwirm went well?"

"Not exactly," said Fliss. "We nearly didn't get out again."

"I did warn you," said Sir Maxim gravely. "However, I'm sorry it wasn't of more use. I hoped she might have let something slip."

"We did find something out," said Pip. "The spirit snatcher's called Octavian – do you know anyone with that name?"

"Sadly not. Then again, I've not lived here long."

He said goodbye and went to join his assistant, who

was sitting in a dark corner, sipping from a glass of port. Shortly afterwards, Seymour and Deathly Graves squirmed through the door and sidled up to the bar. Deathly was limping slightly, while Seymour looked as if one side of him had been flattened – which, of course, it had. Pip clutched his glass of ginger beer nervously as they came up to him.

"So you're thirteen," said Deathly, in her usual downbeat way. "The unluckiest number."

"I'm trying not to think about that," replied Pip.

Seymour was eyeing up a long sticky strip of fly-paper, which hung down from the corner of the bar and was studded with dozens of dead bluebottles. He licked his lips hungrily.

"Isn't there something you need to say to us?" said Fliss. "Like, 'We're really sorry for trying to strangle you the other day'?"

Deathly looked sullen.

"Sorry about that," she muttered, in her low hissing voice. "But what did you expect? We're ghouls. And we've come to make amends."

She looked around for Seymour, but he was too distracted by the fly-paper to join her. Deathly sighed and held out a large box.

"A thirteenth birthday present," she said dolefully. "For both of you. It's not much, but it's all that we have."

"Thanks," said Pip. Behind them, Seymour had started to flail about.

"Mmfh," he said, turning to them and gesturing. "Mmfh!"

The fly-paper spun wildly as Seymour tried to pull away from it, but it was no use. His tongue had become glued to it.

"That's a nasty trick," said Deathly, trying to detach her husband's tongue from the paper. "Who leaves a line of bluebottles out like that if you don't want people to eat them?"

"Glurgh!" screamed Seymour, his eyes bulging as Deathly tugged at the paper. He waved his arms wildly, trying to bat her away, but she was not to be deterred.

"Just hold still," she snapped, and wrenched the fly-paper off Seymour's face. It made a loud, sticky, tearing noise, like ripping off an extra-large plaster.

"AAARGH!" shrieked Seymour and clasped his hands to his mouth, a couple of dead flies still glued to his cheeks. He was staring at Pip and Fliss with tears in his eyes and a horrified expression, as if it was all their fault.

"I wish we'd never bothered coming now," said

Deathly, patting her husband's flattened arm. "Here we are, trying to set things to rights, and you set a trap to tear poor Seymour's tongue off. After all we've suffered."

"You did that to yourselves," said Fliss. "You're just greedy."

"Greedy, are we?" cried Deathly. "We've deprived ourselves, we've come close to starving, just to make amends. Open your present and you'll see."

Pip had a bad feeling about it, but he started to prise the lid off the box.

"Don't…" began Fliss, but it was too late. The lid fell off to reveal thousands of fat brown woodlice. They immediately started to swarm over the sides of the box in a desperate bid for freedom.

"There you are," said Deathly, with the air of someone who has made a great sacrifice. "There's two and a half thousand of them. I counted."

Pip tried to cram the lid back onto the box, but one of Fliss's relations knocked his elbow, sending the woodlice flying through the air. They landed on the bar, on the floor and all over everyone who was standing nearby.

Chaos followed. People started to scream. Seymour crawled around on the floor, frantically stuffing woodlice into his mouth. Fliss's father rushed about with a broom, trying to sweep up as many of the insects as possible.

"It was certainly a more imaginative gift than chocolates," said Mr Whipple, appearing at their sides.

"I know which one I prefer," replied Pip, and Fliss gave a snort of laughter as she fished a swimming woodlouse out of her drink.

"How is your project coming along?" asked Mr Whipple in a low voice. "I hope you're not putting yourselves into any danger?"

"We've actually found something out," said Fliss. "We went to speak to another spirit snatcher and the one here is called Octavian, apparently."

Mr Whipple's eyes widened in surprise.

"I'm amazed you're still alive," he squeaked. "Speaking to a spirit snatcher – my dears, you must be more careful."

"Do you know who Octavian is?"

"Sadly not," said Mr Whipple, shaking his head. "I do wish I could be of more help – you shouldn't be doing this alone."

He broke off abruptly as Mr Wells banged a metal tankard on the bar until all the conversation died down.

"We've all gathered here this evening, not just for Halloween but to celebrate the birthdays of my daughter and her friend, our new neighbour Pip Ruskin," he said in his deep voice. "It may be their thirteenth birthdays, but I hope that this year will be a lucky one for both of them. Everyone, raise your glasses to wish Fliss and Pip a very happy birthday."

The entire crowd toasted them and there were several cheers, which turned into a very off-tune rendition of "Happy Birthday". A cake was produced, which was the colour of dark cherries and had the number thirteen on it, surrounded by candles.

"Make a wish!" someone shouted, and Fliss and Pip leaned forwards to blow them out together.

Fliss closed her eyes tightly and Pip knew that she was wishing for the same thing he was – to find and stop the spirit snatcher.

14
After the Party

The party continued late into the night. Fliss's father had done something to the jukebox so that it played song after song without anyone having to put any money in. No one – not even the ghouls – showed any signs of leaving, and the pub seemed to just get fuller and fuller. There were screams of laughter, and singing, and at some point in the evening, huge platters of hot dogs appeared on the bar, to keep everyone going.

"This is fantastic," said Pip, turning to Fliss as he finished his second hot dog. "Thanks for letting me join in – it would've been the worst birthday ever if you hadn't."

"No worries," said Fliss, who was trying to stop Splodge from eating any more of the woodlice that were still scuttling around.

"Look, I've been thinking," she continued. "You should take Splodge this evening. You're in danger now you're thirteen – the spirit snatcher will be after you. Dogs are supposed to be the best kind of protection, remember?"

"But what about you?" said Pip, raising his voice as the music from the jukebox got even louder. People were starting to dance now, pushing some of the tables back against the walls to clear a space.

"I'll be fine," she said. "It's far less likely to come after me. I'm only half-human, remember? Plus, it'd have to get past Dad first – even a spirit snatcher wouldn't mess with him. You're on your own – there's no one to look after you."

"I don't suppose you're ever going to tell me what you are?" said Pip, having to shout in Fliss's ear over the loud music.

"A werewolf," she said, unexpectedly.

"What?" yelled Pip, not sure if he had heard properly.

"WEREWOLF!" she yelled again, then frowned at the noise. "Look, let's go through into the passage, it's a bit quieter in there."

Fliss ducked around the bar into the passageway, and sat down at the foot of the stairs. Splodge settled himself at her feet, and Pip stood in front of them both.

"I'm not joking," said Fliss. She was looking a bit defensive, as if she wasn't sure how he'd react. "Dad's a werewolf. I mean, you can't be that surprised, can you? You've met enough magical beings by now."

"So every time it's a full moon…" Pip trailed off.

"Yep," she said. "He transforms. Usually Mum makes sure that he's bolted into the cellar – he always likes to stay down there until he turns back again. If he gets out, you never know what he'll do. The only thing that stops him is raw meat. We usually keep some in the freezer, just in case. The things you learn when your father's a werewolf."

Pip wasn't sure what to make of it all. It was a shock, finding out your best friend was part-werewolf. But then again, she was still Fliss.

"Do you turn into one too?" he asked. Fliss shook her head.

"No," she said. "Not yet, anyway. It might happen now I'm thirteen though. I'd love to be a proper one. It's pretty cool, you know. It also means you live for ages – at least two centuries. Unless you get killed in a fight, of course – that's how most werewolves go. Mum's praying that I haven't inherited it though – she's hoping her human side's won out. But I don't want to be just human – that's too boring."

Fliss stopped suddenly, clearly realizing who she was speaking to.

"Sorry! No offence – I just meant that I'd rather be a werewolf like Dad."

"It's fine," said Pip weakly.

Fliss peered at him, looking worried now.

"I've freaked you out, haven't I?" she asked. "Every human panics when they first hear about it. Mum did, when Dad first told her. It was bad enough that he was a pub landlord – her family in Jamaica didn't really approve of that to start with – but being a werewolf as well… Luckily for me, she decided to marry him anyway."

She trailed off, and frowned at Pip.

"You've gone really quiet. Are you sure you want to keep hanging around with me? I totally understand if you don't want to."

"Yes," said Pip firmly, and sat down next to her. "I don't care what you are, it doesn't make a difference. You're still one of the nicest people I've ever met."

Fliss made a disbelieving face, but Pip could tell that she was secretly pleased.

* * *

Fliss insisted that Pip take Splodge. He'd tried to refuse, knowing how attached Fliss was to her pet. He also reminded her of what Miss Qwirm had said – that just because spirit snatchers chose not to attack magical beings, it didn't mean they couldn't. Mr Bletchley was proof of that. But Fliss wouldn't listen.

"You've seen the spirit snatcher before, remember?" she said. "It's already tried to have a go at you, it's got your parents, so it's going to want to finish you off. You're the one who's in the most danger."

She handed Splodge's lead to Pip.

"Come back over here first thing in the morning, so I can give him his breakfast," she instructed.

Predictably, Pip's parents didn't notice when their son arrived home with a dog in tow. It was long after midnight, but the television was still flickering in the darkness. Since his mother was allergic to dogs, Pip took Splodge straight up to his room. He fetched him a bowl of water in case he was thirsty, but the terrier simply sprang up onto Pip's bed and curled up on his duvet. Pip got into bed too, his head whirring with thoughts of werewolves and woodlice, and the music and noise of the party still ringing in his ears.

He was certain he'd never be able to get to sleep.

The street light cast a faint light through the curtainless window, and he could see Splodge snoring softly at the end of his bed. As the hours crept by, the noise from The Ragged Hare next door got louder, as Fliss's father turned the remaining revellers out onto the street, and then it gradually died away, until all was silent.

Pip must have dozed off because he suddenly became aware that Splodge was growling. He sat up, trying to calm the terrier, who had spread himself across Pip's legs and was staring at the window.

The spirit snatcher was back.

The misty shape was seeping in through the gaps in the window frame. Pip watched in horror as it gathered and grew into a thick swirling cloud. He waited for it to come towards him but this time, the mist stayed where it was, hovering by the window, as Splodge's growls grew more threatening. The dog was standing over Pip now, his teeth bared at the mysterious shape.

Pip watched the thick column of cloud as it swirled and spiralled. It seemed to hover there for hours, but in reality it couldn't have been for more than a few minutes. Then, miraculously, it began to seep away again, back through the window, and it melted into the night. Fliss was right – having Splodge had worked. He jumped out

185

of bed, trying to see where the spirit snatcher had got to, but it had vanished. Pip tried to squash some of his clothes into the thin gap between the sash windows, in the hopes that it might prevent the thing from getting back in if it came back for another go. He sat bolt upright in bed, keeping watch, until exhaustion finally overcame him and he fell asleep, Splodge nestled in the crook of his arm.

The next morning, he hurried over to the pub as early as he could, bursting to tell Fliss about what had happened during the night. Splodge trotted beside him, his tail waving happily once he realized that they were heading back to The Ragged Hare. The swing doors were shut but not locked, so Pip went inside. Empty glasses were strewn everywhere, the black balloons still bobbed around the ceiling and the floor was covered with flattened woodlice.

"Fliss?" called Pip, as he peered around the bar into the passageway that led to the flat above. "I've brought Splodge back for his breakfast."

There was the sound of heavy footsteps and Fliss's father came down the stairs. Mr Wells looked dreadful. Pip could tell from his face that something was wrong.

"You'd better come up," he said, and his eyes were fixed on Splodge.

Pip followed him up the stairs, wondering if he had come over too early. Fliss was in the sitting room, slumped in one of the armchairs beside the fire.

"Fliss!" said Pip eagerly. "You'll never guess what happened!"

Fliss stared at Pip as if she didn't recognize him. Splodge trotted up to her and pushed his nose into her hand, but she didn't even look at him.

"Are you feeling okay?" asked Pip.

Fliss just shrugged. Pip had never seen her like this. Perhaps she was just tired from the party. Or maybe she was ill. Or worse. A horrible suspicion came into his mind.

"Can't you see what's happened?" snarled her father, who was standing beside her chair, looking as if he was about to tear Pip limb from limb. "She's been spirit-snatched."

Pip felt as if someone had thrown a bucket of cold water over him.

"She can't have been," he croaked. "Fliss?"

But she didn't answer.

"Why didn't she have Splodge with her?" Mr Wells asked Pip.

"She lent him to me," he said. "She said he'd protect me from the spirit snatcher. And he did."

"So it got her instead," said Mr Wells. His voice was gravelly and he was looking extremely angry.

"She was convinced she'd be okay," said Pip flatly. "Because she's not a human, because she's part-werewolf."

Mr Wells closed his eyes, as if trying very hard to keep control of himself.

"Fliss is my daughter, but she's as human as you are," he said finally. "But she'd never admit it. If she'd inherited anything of the werewolf, there'd have been signs of it by now."

Pip felt a rush of pity for Fliss. He hadn't quite realized just how much she'd wanted to be part-werewolf. She had been so determined to believe that she'd inherited her dad's magical powers that she'd put herself in real danger.

"I didn't realize," said Pip. "I shouldn't have taken Splodge."

"No, you shouldn't," said Mr Wells. "If she hadn't been separated from the dog, this would never have happened."

"I'm so sorry," he said, feeling like the worst person in the world. "I didn't think…"

"She was trying to help you," said Mr Wells with a snarl. "That's why it went for her – you two have been poking about, asking too many questions. You don't do that in a place like this. You keep yourself to yourself, that's how creatures like us manage to get along together. I knew you two were up to something, but I turned the other way. I was glad she had a friend of her own age. Places like this hardly ever have kids – she's always been lonely."

Pip couldn't believe what he was hearing. Fliss was the most confident person he'd ever met. It seemed impossible that she might have been lonely too.

"I'm calling a meeting in the pub," Mr Wells continued fiercely. "I don't know who this spirit snatcher is, but it's made a mistake going for my daughter. You come too. I want everyone there so we can spread the message that it has to fix Fliss."

"I don't think that's going to work," said Pip. "Once someone's been spirit-snatched—"

"IT HAS TO!" bellowed Mr Wells. His whole face was flushed with rage and his yellow eyes flashed. A vein bulged ominously on his forehead. Fliss just sat in the armchair, watching him without emotion or interest.

"Just go," said Mr Wells, when he finally calmed down.

"I have to call Fliss's mother and tell her what's happened. Come back at midday – that's the earliest I'll be able to gather people together."

"I'll leave Splodge here," said Pip.

"Take him with you," replied Mr Wells, and he sounded weary now. "Fliss was trying to keep you safe. It might be too late for her, but there's no point in you being attacked too."

Pip didn't know what to do. Not wanting to go back to his flat, he began to walk away from the alley, without any real idea of where he was going. Splodge trotted beside him, happy to be going for a walk, but Pip felt numb with despair. Fliss had been attacked. He couldn't get his head around it. From the start, she'd always been the one who'd come up with the plans, the one who had always been certain that they'd defeat the spirit snatcher. Without her, it all seemed impossible. He felt terrible for what had happened to Fliss, especially as he now realized just how much he had depended on her as a friend. Pip felt more alone than ever.

It was a bleak November morning and drizzling with rain. Pip wasn't wearing a coat, but he didn't care. He headed towards Piccadilly, joining the crowds of people that were jostling across the pavements. The streets were already filling up with shoppers and tourists, who were taking pictures of themselves on their phones and chatting in loud happy voices. At that moment, Pip would have given anything to be one of them, to have nothing to worry about other than where to go for lunch. He wished that his parents had never moved to Elbow Alley. If they had stayed in Norwich, everyone would still be fine. Mr Bletchley would still be drifting about his shop, and Fliss would never have been attacked.

The task ahead of him felt bigger than ever. Even supposing he found out who the spirit snatcher was, what would he do then? It seemed as if the only real option was to destroy it, yet he had no idea how to go about it, or even if he'd be able to do such a thing. He thought of how Fliss had always been so determined to help him, even though she hadn't needed to, and knew that he couldn't give up now, no matter how hopeless it seemed.

By the time he returned, his legs were aching, he was soaked through and his feet were covered in blisters.

Splodge dragged miserably at his lead, almost as tired as Pip as they navigated the many puddles that had formed in the alleyway. As he reached The Ragged Hare he heard the voice of Fliss's father, loud and furious. The meeting had started.

Pip slipped inside, pulling Splodge with him. Nearly everyone he recognized from Elbow Alley was there. Most of them had been at the party the night before, but now the atmosphere was completely different. Everyone was hushed and subdued, as they huddled together, casting nervous glances at each other.

"Have none of you got the guts to come forwards?" snarled Fliss's father. He was standing in front of the bar and looked larger and fiercer than ever. "One of you attacked my daughter."

No one stirred. It was as if they were all holding their breath.

"I swear, if you don't tell me…" he began, but Penny, who had been standing close to the front, gave a hysterical scream.

"We don't know!" she cried. "None of us know! We're all terrified to death wondering which of us is going to be attacked next!"

She flung her arm out, as if to encompass the lot of

them, and her gaze fell on Pip.

"Why not ask him what's going on?" she shrieked. "It all started when his family came to the alley, didn't it? Poor Mr Bletchley was spirit-snatched only a few days afterwards, and we all know that he was friends with your daughter too. It's something to do with him – I know it! Why else did he come to my shop looking for amulets? It's because he knew something that we didn't!"

Pip felt every pair of eyes turn upon him and he wished he could sink through the floor. He had never wanted to be invisible so badly. The mood in the pub was turning now, getting nastier. He could feel them looking at him as if he was an imposter, as if he was the one behind it all.

"Get him out," hissed Deathly and Seymour, speaking together. The two ghouls slithered forwards, their eyes bulging, their greasy lank hair hanging about their faces. They circled Pip, cracking their knuckles.

"He squashed me," said Seymour. "Left me in a crypt to die."

"Only because you tried to strangle me!" yelled Pip. "And you can't die, remember? So don't pretend you were in any danger."

Seymour shrank back, glaring nastily at Pip. There

was a startled silence, but Pip didn't care. There was something rising up inside him – anger at what had happened, mixed with a sudden overwhelming determination to do something about it. His parents couldn't fix it, and neither could Fliss. And looking at the hopeless fury of Fliss's father, he realized that Mr Wells couldn't fix it either. It was down to him.

"Look," Pip cried, addressing the whole crowd. "I don't know why people are being spirit-snatched. I'd no idea you lot even existed until a few weeks ago. I know I'm not like you, and that I don't belong here. But my parents and my best friend – my only friend – have been attacked. I don't know who the spirit snatcher is, but if I find out, I'm going to put an end to them, even if it kills me."

He gazed fiercely at the sea of shocked faces and realized that he meant every word.

He no longer cared if they were staring, or what they thought of him. There was only one thing that was important – helping Fliss and his parents. He was going to hunt down the spirit snatcher, no matter what.

15

Hunting

Pip left the pub, determined not to waste any time. There were plenty of people in Elbow Alley that he still hadn't spoken to – surely one of them would point him towards Octavian.

He decided to start at the café, as Mrs Ramirez seemed to know everybody and was always full of gossip. She had been at his birthday party the night before, but she had been permanently surrounded by her many friends, so he and Fliss hadn't had a chance to speak to her. Although he knew she was a hag, she seemed to be less dangerous than many of the other residents, and always made a point of greeting him whenever they passed in the street.

Just as he neared the café, the bright blue door beside it flew open, and a girl with long red hair dashed out, nearly colliding with him. It was Aisling, the banshee.

"Hello, Pip," she said. He was surprised that she knew his name, but remembered that she'd been in the pub the previous evening.

"You don't know anyone called Octavian, do you?" he asked, desperation making him sound unusually abrupt.

"No," she said, looking puzzled. "Why?"

Pip shrugged and Aisling laughed.

"You're a funny one," she said. "Listen, I've got to go – I've an audition – but I'll see you around, Pip."

She glided off, a tall slim figure, her red hair floating about her. Pip stepped inside the café.

It was busy and noisy – music blared, a coffee machine whirred loudly, and there was a gentle hum of people talking. He had hit the lunchtime rush and there was a long line of men in suits and smartly dressed women queuing up for toasted sandwiches and salads and burritos – Mrs Ramirez's café was popular with the workers from the nearby offices.

Pip and Splodge sidled up the side of the queue, ignoring the tutting noises and annoyed frowns of the other customers. Mrs Ramirez was somehow managing to make a number of complicated coffees and take people's money, while preparing about forty different sandwiches at once. It was incredible to watch her.

She moved so fast she was almost blurred.

"What would you like?" she asked, as Pip reached the counter, then she did a double take when she realized it was him.

"Pip!" she cried, already looking over his shoulder to take the next person's order. "What is going on? I heard that Edgar had called a meeting in the pub, but it's been too busy for me to leave the café."

She beckoned for him to come around to the other side of the counter.

"Tell me everything," she said. "And while you are here, could you watch the sandwich toaster?"

She nodded to an enormous metal griddle which contained several dozen sandwiches in varying degrees of toastiness.

"The spirit snatcher got Fliss," said Pip flatly, as he lifted the lid of the griddle and prodded at the nearest sandwich, sending cheese oozing out of the sides.

"No!" cried Mrs Ramirez, and stopped what she was doing for a split second to stare at Pip in horror. "The poor girl."

She made the sign of the cross, then caught sight of the ever-growing queue, and turned reluctantly back to the coffee machine.

"Mrs Ramirez," said Pip. "Do you know anyone in the alley called Octavian?"

"Octavian?" she repeated, raising her voice above the sound of the milk frother. "I don't. But I do know an Octavia."

"You do?" said Pip. Perhaps they had misheard Melody, perhaps she had been saying Octavia all along. He was thinking so hard that he didn't even notice that the sandwiches were starting to burn.

"Yes, Octavia," said Mrs Ramirez. "She owns the hat shop, just next door. She's very nice. We go for dinner, her sisters too, every month. So funny."

"Thanks!" said Pip, as plumes of smoke began to rise up from the back of the griddle. Mrs Ramirez gave an alarmed sniff as the burning smell spread across the shop, then rushed across to rescue the over-toasted sandwiches, almost falling over Splodge, who had been hoovering up the crumbs on the floor.

"Wait!" she cried as Pip began to hurry off. "You didn't say why you were looking for her."

"I can't tell you yet," said Pip, as he weaved his way through the queue and out the door. "Sorry about the sandwiches!"

* * *

Pip had never really noticed the hat shop before. Compared to the black velvet draperies of Past Caring or the cluttered windows of Dribs & Drabs, it looked quite ordinary by comparison. A set of plaster busts sat in the window, each one wearing a different sort of hat. They ranged from a man's bowler in black silk with an upturned brim, to a peachy-pink fascinator which was decorated with several long flamingo feathers. The shopfront was painted an olive green and the words *Shuttleworth & Sisters* were written above it in faded gold letters. It didn't seem like the type of place where an evil spirit snatcher would live – it looked like a shop where you'd buy a hat for a wedding.

Pip pressed the doorbell. There was a buzzing noise and the door clicked open.

"Come on, Splodge," he muttered to the terrier. "Let's see what Octavia's like."

The inside of the shop was gloomy, like all the other shops in the alley, although large mirrors were set into the walls. In the centre of the shop were several more displays of hats, propped up on long thin sticks so they seemed to hover in the air at eye level. A high shelf ran around the top of the room, and on it were stacked piles of olive-green hatboxes.

However, Pip's attention was drawn to the long wall behind the counter. It was covered in hundreds of sheets of paper, each of which was marked with a pattern of tiny holes that traced a roundish shape. They were all a little different – some of them were almost circular, others were long and oval. He moved closer to get a better look, and saw that each sheet had a different person's name written on it. Many of them were old and yellowed, as if they dated back many years, while some of them looked as if they had been made very recently.

"They're templates of head shapes," said a high voice. "Everyone notices them when they come in."

A tiny woman appeared out of the shadows, so suddenly that Pip jumped.

"They're taken from our customers," she continued. "Exact measurements of their skull. Hardly anyone else can do it so accurately. It's our speciality."

She gave Pip a piercing stare.

"I know who you are," she said. "I was at your birthday party. And my sister has just told me all about what happened at Edgar Wells's meeting. You're Pip Ruskin, the boy behind all the recent…excitement."

Her voice was a bit unsettling. It was very girlish and soft, the sort of voice that should belong to a shy five year old. But this woman was quite old – her face was papery and lined, and her brown hair was streaked with silver.

"Are you Octavia?" asked Pip.

"I'm Annabelle," the woman replied. "But Octavia's just out the back.

"Ottie!" she called, in her high breathless voice. "There's a boy here to see you."

"A boy?" Another woman seemed to materialize from thin air. She looked so similar to Annabelle that they had to be related.

"This is my sister Sybil," said Annabelle.

"Oh," said Sybil, looking at Pip, clearly disappointed. "He really is a boy. I thought you meant someone more grown up."

"Sybil, you are impossible," said Annabelle, and broke into a tinkling laugh. She stopped abruptly when a third identical figure appeared.

"This is Ottie…I mean Octavia," she said.

"You're the boy who's hunting the spirit snatcher," said Octavia, staring at him. Even though she looked and sounded the same as her sisters, she carried herself with more authority. Pip suddenly realized that he had no idea what to do next. He could hardly ask if she was the spirit snatcher, not when he was standing in her shop, surrounded by her sisters – it would be incredibly stupid.

"Yes," he said. "I'm just asking around, trying to see if anyone knows anything."

Octavia's expression did not change, she simply continued to stare unblinkingly at Pip. It made Pip feel extremely awkward and a little dizzy.

"I don't want to cause any trouble," he said hurriedly. "I just want to make Fliss and my parents go back to normal. And Mr Bletchley too," he added, as an afterthought.

"Of course you do," she said. "You want information. But I think we'd like to know some information about you first."

"I'm Pip Ruskin," began Pip. "I'm thirteen and I used to live in—"

"Not that kind of information," laughed Annabelle.

"Silly boy," giggled Sybil, and she dabbed at her eyes with a lacy handkerchief.

"She means we want to get the measure of you," said Annabelle, and she pointed at the wall of paper templates.

"You can learn everything about a person from the shape of their head," said Octavia. "If you know how to go about it."

"And we do!" shrilled Sybil.

"Shall we get the contraption?" asked Annabelle.

"Yes," said Octavia. "The contraption is exactly what we need."

Sybil dived into the room at the back of the shop.

"I'm fine," said Pip, backing away. "Whatever the contraption is, I really don't want to—"

"You will be measured," said Octavia. "It won't take a minute."

Sybil reappeared, holding a round leather box. It was so large that it hid her face, and she staggered slightly under its weight.

Annabelle meanwhile had circled round to the other side of Pip and had produced a chair.

"Why don't you sit down?" she said, pressing Pip's shoulder.

"I'd rather not," said Pip, who was regretting coming into the shop at all. He began to think that the best plan would be to make a run for it. Whatever was in that box, he didn't want it anywhere near him.

But Annabelle's hand, although it was small and frail, was surprisingly strong. She tightened her grip on Pip's shoulder and pushed him downwards with incredible strength, until he was sitting on the chair. Sybil and Octavia were carefully lifting the contraption out of the box. It looked like an enormous metal spider with thick steel legs that were waving about. Octavia carried it over, cradling it in her arms, while Sybil spread a large sheet of paper across the pitted surface of the counter.

"Get off me," yelled Pip, trying to twist away from Annabelle. "Don't you bring that thing any closer."

"Stay still," instructed Octavia. "It will hurt less that way."

"Splodge!" yelled Pip, hoping that the terrier would come to his rescue.

But although Splodge whined and scrabbled at his legs, the sisters continued to advance upon him.

"Splodge," called Pip again. "Do something!"

"The dog won't touch us," said Annabelle. "We're not doing you any harm."

"Just be still," repeated Octavia, and the metal contraption sprang out of her arms and fastened itself on top of Pip's head.

He yelled and tried to grasp the long pincered legs that were digging themselves into his skull, but Annabelle and Sybil had each grabbed hold of one of his arms. They were dragging him down, forcing him to stay put. The spidery legs were tapping around the edges of his skull, hard enough to be painful, and there was a strange feeling in his brain, as if all his memories were whirling about. He tried to stop it, to bring his mind back to the present, but they just sped around faster than ever, until he felt sick at the speed of it. Suddenly, the metal spider leaped off his head and landed on top of the counter, where it began to stab holes in the sheet of paper, forming an exact impression of the shape of Pip's head. It made another set of impressions too, fainter marks like Braille which left dents instead of holes, and formed an intricate pattern that bloomed within the dotted outline of Pip's skull.

"It's tracing what's going on inside your brain," said Sybil, helpfully.

Pip stared at the machine in horror. It continued tapping away creating an ever more complicated pattern, then it abruptly collapsed in a heap on the counter, as if whatever had been propelling it had turned itself off.

"There," said Octavia, and she nodded to her sisters, who let Pip go at once. He immediately reached up to rub his temples, trying to figure out if it had done anything to him.

"You'll be quite all right," said Octavia. "It's got the measure of you, that's all."

"The good news is that we have your precise head

shape," said Annabelle. "If you'd ever like to buy a hat."

"Would you like a sweet?" said Sybil, holding out a box of marzipan fruits. "Some customers take the measuring worse than others."

Pip refused the marzipan. He was more interested in Octavia, who had returned the contraption to its box and was now carefully studying the sheet of paper.

"I see there's a lot going on in your head, Pip Ruskin," she said. "You never wanted to come here, did you?"

"No," said Pip.

"And you are more upset by what happened to your parents than you let on. You've spent your life being ashamed of them, and now you would give anything to have them back."

Pip said nothing.

"You are trying to stop the spirit snatcher, but you have no idea what to do if you find it. You think it's a hopeless quest, but you don't know what else you can do."

She paused, then continued in the same even tone.

"And for the last ten minutes, you have been convinced that I am the spirit snatcher."

She gazed inscrutably at Pip, while her sisters giggled nervously. Pip's insides squirmed.

"I am not the spirit snatcher," she said at last. "My

sisters and I are sylphs – we are spirits of the air, the three graces."

She flicked her hands outwards and for a moment all the hats in the shop rose up and hovered in the air, their ribbons and veils fluttering. Splodge started barking, Pip gasped, and Annabelle and Sybil started giggling at the shocked expression on his face. Octavia gave a small smile, then dropped her hands to her sides. The hats fell back into their places at once, limp and lifeless.

For a moment, Pip simply sat there, too stunned to move.

"Do you believe me now?"

"Yes," he said, at last, experiencing a curious mixture of disappointment and relief. He no longer thought that he was about to be spirit-snatched, but he felt as if he had come to yet another dead end.

"I don't suppose you know who the spirit snatcher is?" he asked.

"I don't," said Octavia. "As far as I know, I have never met it."

Annabelle and Sybil both agreed, fluttering round their sister, who was looking thoughtful.

"But I can tell you from what I saw in your head that you heard that poor girl Melody correctly," she said finally. "She did say that the spirit snatcher was called Octavian."

As Pip stood up to leave, Annabelle and Sybil fussed around him, offering him yet more marzipan and enquiring how he was feeling in the aftermath of the measuring. Although he felt as if his investigations hadn't moved on very much, it was comforting to know that at least he had made a few new allies in Elbow Alley, and had uncovered more of its hidden magic.

16

The Full Moon Rises

Pip staggered out of the hat shop, his brain still spinning slightly. He wasn't certain where to go next, so after checking on his parents, he wandered over to see Mr Whipple, hoping for some guidance. The bookseller took one look at Pip's weary expression and insisted he sit down in one of the comfortable leather armchairs.

"It's impossible," said Pip, stroking Splodge, who had curled himself up on his lap. "I thought I was getting somewhere."

"Well, you've certainly set yourself a challenge," sighed the bookseller, coming over with two steaming mugs of milky tea and a plate of sandwiches.

"You should eat something," he said, as he handed Pip a mug and sat down in the other armchair. "You look exhausted."

"Thanks," said Pip gratefully.

Julius came in, stopped dead when he saw Pip, then turned and went back into the storeroom. Pip was relieved – Julius's silent presence always made him feel uncomfortable.

"Are you sure you've never come across someone called Octavian?" Pip asked, lowering his voice so there was no chance the assistant would hear him.

"I'm afraid not," replied Mr Whipple, taking a sip of his tea. "And I've lived here for ten years."

"Perhaps he keeps a really low profile," suggested Pip, taking another sandwich. "You might've never seen him."

"That's quite possible," agreed Mr Whipple pleasantly. "I've no idea who lives in some of these buildings. Take the one opposite, for instance."

He pointed through the window at the shabby old house across the street. It had a thick layer of dust on the windows and faded stained curtains. Pip thought that it definitely looked like the sort of place where someone might choose to hide.

"I'll check it out," he said. "I'm going to keep knocking on doors, see if I can find anything out. If I can just find the spirit snatcher, I might be able to get some of the other people in Elbow Alley to help me stop it."

"I'd really advise against it," said Mr Whipple, sounding worried. "You could come to a tremendous amount of harm. Although I see you're looking after Splodge."

He gave the terrier a sharp look, but Pip wasn't listening. He set Splodge back down on the ground, got to his feet and wandered over to the *Occult* section beside the counter. Splodge followed his every move, as if he was joined to Pip by an invisible thread. He was clearly missing Fliss.

"There must be *something* about spirit snatchers," muttered Pip, pulling out *Odd and Awful Creatures of the British Isles* and flicking through it. There was an entry on salamanders and another on swamp monkeys, but nothing on spirit snatchers. He replaced it, looking about for something more useful, and then his eye fell on the shelf of books behind the counter. He went over to it, scanning the titles. There, wedged in between several volumes of *Tales of the Strange and Occult* was a very slender book, bound in worn green leather, with the words *Spirit Snatchers* glimmering on the spine in golden curling letters.

Pip seized it at once, and opened it.

Of all the magical creatures, the spirit snatcher is the most dangerous to humans as it feeds on their spirits, which is widely believed to be an even worse fate than consuming their flesh. Once a spirit snatcher transforms its body into mist and fastens itself upon an unfortunate victim, it will drain their spirit away, never to be returned, leaving naught but the physical body behind. The spirit snatcher stays in the shadows and is so powerful that there is little chance of stopping it. The only possible way is to use the spirit snatcher's own power against it, which is why a spirit snatcher in its vaporous form is loath to confront its own reflection in the light. In 1740, there was the example of Abraxas Dean, who once hunted down a legendary spirit snatcher by the name of Montgomery Stillwell…

Then a shadow fell across the pages. Pip glanced up and saw Julius looming over him. He looked around wildly for Mr Whipple, hoping that the bookseller would come to his aid, but Julius had already wrenched the book out of his hands and returned it to the shelf.

"Get out," said Julius.

"Oh dear," said Mr Whipple, who was hovering by the

counter, looking alarmed. "Pip, I really think you'd better go."

"But the book!" protested Pip. "Can I borrow it? It's all about spirit snatchers."

"I'm afraid the books behind the counter are reserved for customers," said Mr Whipple, wringing his hands and looking from Julius to Pip. "Somebody must have ordered it. Did they, Julius?"

Julius didn't answer, he just stared at Mr Whipple and didn't say a word. Mr Whipple met his gaze for a moment, then ushered Pip and Splodge out of the shop. It seemed as if Mr Whipple was very keen to avoid any sort of confrontation with his assistant.

"Leave this with me, Pip," he said. "I'll find out who reserved the book. Perhaps that's the clue to this mystery."

"How long will it take you?" asked Pip.

"I'll send word as soon as I can," promised the bookseller. "But perhaps you should return Fliss's dog. She's more on her own than ever, since her father's been spirit-snatched."

"What?" Pip stared at Mr Whipple in shock. "Fliss's father had his spirit taken as well?"

"Shortly after the meeting, I believe. Apparently he

had gone into the pub's cellar and was attacked in there. It's most unusual for something like this to happen during daylight hours, so I really think this should be a warning to you, Pip. You should leave Elbow Alley before it gets you too."

But Pip wasn't listening. He was too concerned about Fliss and her father.

"So who's looking after them now?" he asked.

"I'm not sure," replied Mr Whipple, looking troubled. "As you can imagine, everyone is terrified that they will be the next victim."

"I've got to go," said Pip, determined to get to The Ragged Hare without delay. "Let me know when you find out about the book – it's really important. I've got to read it."

He glanced over at Julius, who was still standing guard over the bookshelf as if he was ready to kill Pip if he took so much as another step towards it.

"I will, Pip," promised Mr Whipple, as he glanced over at Julius, a curious expression on his face.

Darkness had fallen by the time Pip left the bookshop. A bright full moon stood out against the inky sky, and the air was cold and sharp. Splodge growled and Pip saw that there was a rat watching him again. Pip was certain it was the same one he'd seen before. Splodge barked and the rat scuttled off, disappearing through the crack beneath the door of the abandoned house. As he reached The Ragged Hare he heard a smashing noise coming from within.

Inside, the pub looked as if it had been burgled. The chairs and tables had been tossed across the floor. Some of them had their legs ripped off, while the bar stools had their stuffing spilling out of the seats as if someone had taken an enormous bite out of each one. The mirror behind the bar was shattered into a million minuscule fragments, while all the shelves were empty as hundreds of glasses lay smashed on the ground, in a vast mound of glittering shards. Pip was beginning to feel distinctly nervous, but he was determined to see if Fliss was okay.

He took a deep breath and stepped through the door at the side of the bar, into the passageway. There was another smash from overhead. He took a deep breath and went up the stairs. Fliss was sitting in a chair beside the fireplace, but there was no fire burning. The room was dark and chilly, the curtains open.

"Are you okay?" asked Pip urgently. "What happened?"

Fliss said nothing and carried on staring into space, as if he wasn't there. There was another loud smash, and Pip realized it was coming from the kitchen.

He edged towards the kitchen door. There was a strange noise – a scrunching, grinding sound. Splodge was following him, so close he could feel the dog pressing against his leg. Pip stepped through the door and froze.

He was face to face with an enormous snarling werewolf.

It was as large as a bear, with jet-black fur and enormous yellow eyes. As soon as it saw Pip, it reared up on its hind legs and advanced towards him, roaring. The floor was covered with smashed plates and bowls, and Pip realized that the grating sound he had heard was the sound of the broken china crunching under the werewolf's big paws.

For a moment, Pip found himself unable to move. He was hypnotized by the beast's yellow eyes, by its long pointed teeth. Then Splodge started barking madly, distracting it. Pip backed out of the kitchen and slammed the door shut. Splodge stopped barking at once and raced over to Fliss.

The moonlight was shining through the window and Pip suddenly knew what had happened. If Mr Wells had been spirit-snatched, he wouldn't have thought to shut himself up in the cellar, and Fliss was in no state to help him either. Presumably being spirit-snatched only affected the human part of him – the animal side certainly seemed to be in possession of its full senses. There was a loud thud as the werewolf flung itself at the door and Pip jumped back. The wood splintered and buckled. Another thud and the door was torn off its hinges, and the werewolf burst out of the kitchen. When it saw the moonlight, it threw back its head and gave a loud howl, then bounded away, leaping down the stairs in a single powerful spring.

"We've got to stop him," cried Pip. "He'll kill someone."

He grabbed Fliss's shoulders and gazed into her eyes desperately.

"What should I do? Fliss?"

It was no use – she didn't seem to hear him. Pip racked his brains, trying to remember what Fliss had said about her father. Then it came back to him. He dashed back into the kitchen and yanked open the freezer. There in the top drawer was a huge leg of uncooked lamb. Pip grabbed it and raced after Mr Wells, Splodge hot on his heels. He almost slid down the stairs and shot across the pub, jumping over the fallen chairs, then he skidded out into the alley.

It was empty. Pip looked up and down the street, trying to figure out which way Fliss's father had gone. Then, a table smashed through the window of Dribs & Drabs and crashed down into the street, glass scattering everywhere. Pip could hear Penny's screams as he sprinted up the alley towards it, Splodge racing ahead. The shop door was standing open. Penny was pressed against the wall at the back of the shop, cornered by the huge, snarling werewolf.

Pip had grown so used to seeing Penny wrapped up in her long coat that he had almost forgotten she was a harpy. She wasn't hiding now, but fighting the werewolf with all her strength. Penny's familiar face and sausage curls looked faintly ridiculous, perched on top of the feathered body of a huge eagle. The sight was made still stranger by the fact that she had a pair of human arms, alongside a pair of wings that she must have kept tucked away under her voluminous clothing. Now, those wings were flapping, causing Penny to hover a few feet off the ground. She was striking out at the werewolf with her talons, but even so, Pip could see that she was at a disadvantage. Her poky shop was so full of clutter that she didn't have the space to fly or even free herself. She was stuck in one corner, and although her claws were sharp, the werewolf had claws too, as well as a set of long sharp teeth. It looked as though it was about to tear her apart.

"Hey!" yelled Pip, charging into the shop. "Leave her alone."

The werewolf's ears flicked back, but it didn't turn around.

Pip spotted the entrance to Penny's basement storeroom out of the corner of his eye and an idea came into his head.

"Look!" he called again, and moved forwards, holding the leg of lamb out like a baton. "I've got something for you."

The werewolf caught sight of the meat and its eyes gleamed. It roared again, but less ferociously this time. Penny struck out again with her talons.

"Don't," said Pip in a low voice. The last thing he needed was for the werewolf to become even angrier. He carried on waving the lamb and edged towards the open storeroom door. He waited until the werewolf was so close that he could smell its rotting breath, then he flung the frozen meat down the dark stairs, hearing it clunk all the way down to the room below. The werewolf leaped down the stairs after it.

Pip slammed the door shut and turned the key in the lock.

"Quick!" he said to Penny. "Help me move the furniture in front of the door. It'll never hold if he tries to smash through it."

He started to push at a large dresser, the china rattling as it juddered across the floor. Penny, who had folded her wings away and put her coat back on, lifted the other side and together they moved it in front of the storeroom door. They dragged a couple of heavy oak chests over too and stacked them up in front of the dresser to create a solid barrier.

"Hopefully that'll stop him," said Pip. "Or at least slow him down a bit."

Penny was breathing very heavily and was holding her hand to her chest.

"I thought I was going to die," she said faintly. "My poor heart, the shock of it. There I was, just sitting in the shop, and before I knew it, that *thing* was tearing the place up. It's never happened before, never in my entire life and I'm three hundred years old next spring. To attack a fellow creature, without any good reason. I don't care if he was a werewolf, it's still not right."

"Mr Wells was spirit-snatched," said Pip. "It wasn't his fault."

"That horrible spirit snatcher," she shrieked, and she was weeping now, fat tears rolling down her face and falling into her feathers. "It's destroying everything. I'm not staying here. As soon as I find a new place to live, I'm leaving."

"It'll be all right," said Pip, trying to calm her down. Other people were arriving now – Deathly and Seymour had arrived, Julius was lurking by the doorway, not speaking to anyone, and then Sir Maxim appeared, looking grave.

"What happened?" he asked. "I heard the noise."

"It's Fliss's dad," said Pip. "Don't worry – he's locked in the storeroom."

Penny started to tell her story to the growing crowd. Pip went outside and retrieved the table that had been thrown through the window.

"And he saved me," concluded Penny, as Pip came back in with the table. Everyone stared at him, but Pip found that he didn't mind a bit. It was a very different thing to be noticed for having done something brave.

Penny went over to the glass cabinet and opened it.

"Have this," she said, picking up a little piece of shiny metal and holding it out to Pip. It was the amulet.

"It's all right," he said, shaking his head.

"No, I insist," said Penny. "I know how much you wanted it."

"I don't need it now," he said. "I shouldn't have taken it in the first place."

"It was yours by right anyway," insisted Penny. "I knew it was unfair to go back on my side of the deal. But please, take it now, as a thank you."

Pip slipped it into his coat pocket.

"It isn't a proper amulet, though," she added in an undertone, so that no one else could hear. "Just in case you were thinking of using it for anything. I got it as part of a job lot of junk. Utterly useless. But it looks quite pretty, with the mirrored back."

"Thanks," said Pip. He smiled at Penny and she patted him on the shoulder in a positively friendly way.

Mr Wells was still in the cellar. Either he was still chewing at the meat or he had decided to stay put for the time being, but either way, Pip was thankful that he'd gone silent. Feeling that the presence of a vampire, a harpy and several ghouls would be more than enough to restrain the werewolf if he tried to fight his way out, Pip slipped away to check on Fliss.

Fliss was still sitting exactly where he had left her. In a way, she seemed to be in an even worse state than his parents – she didn't want to eat anything, and shook her head when Pip offered her a glass of water. The only thing she did was to clasp Splodge tightly when the terrier jumped up into her lap.

Pip stayed with her for a while, but it was obvious that she barely registered his presence. A tremendous sense of rage was beginning to bubble up inside Pip. It seemed that everyone he cared about had fallen prey to the spirit snatcher. It was getting late but he had no intention of going to bed. He had been thinking a lot about what he had read in that old book in Mr Whipple's shop. A spirit snatcher needed to transform in order to attack, but it was also at its most vulnerable when it assumed its vaporous form. Then something occurred to him. The book had said quite clearly that the spirit snatcher didn't like the light and every single incident that had happened in Elbow Alley had occurred overnight. The only person who hadn't been attacked overnight was Mr Wells, but hadn't Mr Whipple said that he'd been in the pub's dark cellar when the spirit snatcher found him? There was barely any light in there – it would have been the perfect setting for the spirit snatcher. Pip immediately turned on every single overhead light that he could, feeling that he had made a breakthrough, then hunted about Fliss's flat until he found what he was looking for – a torch. He tried it, to make sure it was working, and a dazzlingly strong beam shone across the sitting room, far better than the feeble one he had on his phone.

Pip suddenly felt extremely confident. There was something about the light that the spirit snatcher avoided. He would confront the spirit snatcher, then when it took on its misty form – as it would have to do if it wanted to attack him – he would blast it with the torch. That should have the effect of turning it back against itself, as the book said.

He would wait with Fliss and Splodge until dawn, and then, if the spirit snatcher hadn't come for him by then, he would hunt it down, armed with his new knowledge that the creature couldn't attack him in the light. Either there was some way for it to return everyone's spirits, or else he would destroy it with the torch. He didn't feel the least bit of apprehension now – just a grim determination at what he needed to do.

17

The Shapeshifter

The spirit snatcher did not appear that night. Perhaps it was because Pip was willing it to, or perhaps it was simply unaware that he was in The Ragged Hare instead of his own home. Pip was too on edge to sleep much, even with the protective presence of Splodge close by, and he had already eaten breakfast and was ready to get started by the time the first glimmer of daylight finally appeared.

"I'm going out," he said to Fliss. She didn't even look at him. She just sat there, clutching Splodge tightly.

Pip wondered if he should take the dog with him, but Splodge refused to leave Fliss and Fliss seemed equally reluctant to let go of Splodge. So he went on his own, torch clutched firmly in his hand, ready to track down the spirit snatcher.

Elbow Alley was not a long street, and Pip reasoned

that there weren't many places where the spirit snatcher could be hiding. But there was one, very obvious place he had missed – the large, derelict building that stood opposite the café and Mr Whipple's bookshop. The more Pip thought about it, the more he was certain that this was its lair. No one seemed to know anything about it, he had never seen anyone go in or out, and yet it stood right in the middle of the alleyway, perfectly placed for the spirit snatcher to watch everything that was going on. They'd been right outside that house when Mrs Ruskin had dropped her suitcase, that first afternoon when they were moving in. It was only two doors down from Mr Bletchley's shop and diagonally across from The Ragged Hare, and he could see the house if he stuck his head out of his bedroom window. It would take a spirit snatcher no time at all to mist its horrible way around the street.

Pip went up the alley, shivering in the biting wind that whistled down the narrow street. The sky had already clouded over and it started to rain, lightly at first, but getting steadily heavier.

The derelict house was a large building, several storeys high, and looked as if nobody had lived there for many years. Pip rapped the old iron knocker, then rattled the locked door. He bent down and peered through the letter box, but all he could see was a dusty wooden staircase in the gloom within. As he did so, he felt his spine prickle. Someone was watching him. He straightened up and looked around, but could see no one.

Then Pip noticed something. Behind the grimy window, one of the old stained curtains was swaying very gently, as if someone had just brushed past it. He peered through the glass, but the room inside was completely bare. Pip placed his hands on the window frame and tried to pull up the sash, but it wouldn't budge. He stepped back and looked up at the house. To his surprise, there was now a faint light shining from one of the attic rooms. He examined the old metal drainpipes, wondering if he could climb up them, but decided that it was impossible. The rain grew heavier, and from somewhere close by came the rumble of thunder.

Pip knocked at the door once more, clutching to the faint hope that whoever was inside might let him in, but there was no response. He tried the handle again. This time, when he turned the old iron knob, the door creaked open.

"Hello?" called Pip, looking about nervously. He was quite certain that the door had been locked before.

Someone must be lurking, just out of sight. Pip clutched his torch, ready to turn it on if needed, then stepped into the house, his nerves crackling with anticipation. It smelt musty and stale. Everything was coated with a thick layer of dust that rose up in clouds with every step he took, sticking to his damp clothes. He headed towards the staircase, and although every instinct was telling him to turn and run, he forced himself to start climbing up. The wooden treads creaked with every step he took, sounding incredibly loud. Whatever was waiting for him would know that he was coming. Pip carried on past the first floor and up to the second. At the top of the stairs he paused, feeling as if he was going to be sick. There, in front of him, was a closed door, with a chink of light spilling out beneath.

Pip had no idea what was behind it. For one wild moment he thought about turning around, of running down the stairs and getting out of the house as fast as possible. But if he did that, he'd never be able to live with himself. He was so close to unravelling the mystery, there was no going back now. And the spirit snatcher was hunting him anyway. It was far better for him to confront it first. He knew that was what Fliss would do.

Pip took a deep breath and turned the tarnished brass

handle. His heart thudded wildly as he stepped inside. There was no one there. A single bare light bulb hung from the ceiling and the walls were covered in a patterned wallpaper, in swirls of purples and browns and oranges. There was no furniture at all – the room was completely empty. Pip made his way over to the window, his knees feeling weak with relief, but even as he did so, he felt someone watching him. He whirled around and caught sight of something that almost made him cry out with shock. Two eyes were blinking out at him from the wallpaper.

As Pip stared in horror at the pair of disembodied eyes, the wallpaper seemed to bulge and move, and he saw that a figure was standing there. It was the size and shape of a man, but it was completely concealed in the wallpaper pattern, from its face to its feet, its eyes the only things that were visible.

"Who are you?" croaked Pip.

The creature blinked a couple of times, then it swirled around and changed form, into an exact copy of Pip, right down to the clothes he was wearing.

If the eyes were bad, this was much worse. Pip felt as if he was looking at himself in a mirror, except his reflection was moving around without him. It was so unnerving, being confronted by himself, that he backed away towards the door.

"Don't go," his mirror image said in a whispery voice. "I didn't mean to startle you."

And it changed again, into a man that Pip had not seen before. He was thin and grey-faced and seemed as shadowy as a ghost, wearing an old-fashioned overcoat.

"Who are you?" said Pip, trying to keep his voice steady. The man seemed to shrink away from Pip, as if he didn't want to be seen.

"I'm…Mapullan," said the man at last, stumbling over his own name.

"You're the spirit snatcher?" said Pip. His hand closed around his torch, getting ready to blast it with a beam of light, even though, now he thought about it, the presence of the light bulb made the torch somewhat unnecessary.

But the man was shaking his head.

"I'm…not," he said.

"I've been looking for you for days," said Pip. "It all fits."

"I p…promise I'm not," said the man. He was blushing and Pip suddenly realized that whatever this man was, he was incredibly shy, as if he could not bear Pip to notice him.

"What are you then?" asked Pip.

In response, the man turned into a rat.

"I'm a shapeshifter," he said. His voice was the same, but it seemed to be steadier now, and didn't stutter, as if he was more comfortable in a rat's body than in his own. "I've been watching you since you first arrived in Elbow Alley."

"Why?" said Pip, feeling more confused than ever as he looked into the rat's beady little eyes.

"I see everything, but no one sees me," said Mapullan. "It is how it's always been. I have known this place for centuries. I have seen people come, and I have seen people go."

"And you live here?" said Pip, still unnerved by the atmosphere of the austere, abandoned house.

"I move about," said Mapullan. "I never stay too long. It attracts attention, you see, staying in one place. I very rarely reveal myself."

"Would you mind turning back into a person again?" asked Pip. He was finding it quite surreal, talking to a rat.

There was a *swoosh* and the young man reappeared, blinking and pulling his overcoat about him, as if he was trying to hide himself.

"It is very rare for a shapeshifter to appear in its human form," said Mapullan. "It costs us a great effort. The only reason I chose to reveal myself to you is because I sensed in you a kindred spirit."

"You did?" said Pip, surprised.

"From the moment I saw you," he said. "I could tell that you always wished to blend in. As a shapeshifter, you can. You have the power to move through the world without ever being noticed. Why don't you join me? I would be glad of some company. I can pass on the gift, if you choose it."

Mapullan's face was eager as he looked at Pip, his shyness falling away for a moment.

"I'm sorry," said Pip. "I used to wish that my parents would be like everyone else, that I'd just be able to go through life without anybody noticing me. But I don't really care about that any more. I just want my parents and my friend back."

Mapullan looked as if Pip had stabbed him.

"I only ask out of the purest motives," he said. "You are in danger. If you don't conceal yourself, you will be spirit-snatched before much longer. It's a miracle that you have survived this long."

"I can't hide myself away," said Pip firmly. "I've got to

fix what's been done to everyone. I'd rather be attacked than not do anything. Unless…"

An idea had occurred to him.

"Can I become a shapeshifter temporarily?" he asked. "I'd have a much better chance of stopping the spirit snatcher, and I'd love to be able to change into anything I wanted."

"That isn't possible," said Mapullan softly. "Once you become a shapeshifter you must spend your life living in the shadows. You cannot live among others. It is the price you must pay."

"In that case, I can't do it," said Pip. He was beginning to feel sorry for Mapullan but he couldn't abandon his friends and family.

The sound of singing drifted up from the street outside. It was melodic and beautiful, but Pip thought that it was the saddest sound he had ever heard. He looked out of the window and saw Aisling walking down the alley, seemingly unaware of the rain, singing as she went.

"A banshee's song," said Mapullan, joining Pip at the window. "You know what that means."

Pip shook his head.

"It means that somebody is about to die."

Pip looked down at Aisling, who had paused outside the blue door of her flat to finish her song, then disappeared inside. There was a long silence as they both stared at the place where she had been.

"Do you have any idea who the spirit snatcher is?" asked Pip.

"I know where it lives," said Mapullan. "Night after night, as I watch from this window, I see where the dark mist appears from. I have seen it go through your bedroom window many times in the hope of finding you alone. It is hunting you – you must know that by now. If you stayed here, became a shapeshifter, you would be safe."

"Where does it live?" asked Pip urgently. "Where does the mist come from?"

In response, Mapullan pointed at the window, towards the building that stood right in front of them.

"The bookshop," whispered Pip and Mapullan nodded.

Pip was thinking rapidly. He'd been so preoccupied with finding someone called Octavian that he had never really considered Julius, but he had been the obvious suspect all along. He thought of the sullen, scowling assistant, who always looked as if he'd like nothing better than to suck the life out of anyone who crossed his path. He lived in the bookshop – Mr Whipple had mentioned that he occupied one of the upstairs rooms. Julius was also the only person in the alley, apart from Pip and his family, who didn't seem to have any connection to the magical community here and kept himself apart from everyone. Mr Whipple seemed strangely nervous of him, as if he knew something unpleasant about his odd employee. Then, there was the biggest clue of all – the way that he had prevented Pip from reading that book. There was probably no customer waiting for it – it was just Julius. Maybe Octavian was his surname.

"It's been him all along," he muttered. "I've been so stupid. I should have thought of him before."

"Be very careful," said Mapullan. "No one has ever managed to overcome a spirit snatcher. You should flee."

"I'm not doing that," said Pip firmly. "I'm going over there to stop him."

"Don't," said the shapeshifter. He reached forwards and tugged at the sleeve of Pip's coat. "The home of a spirit snatcher is no place for a person as spirited as you."

But Pip shook him off and hurried towards the door.

"Thanks for your help!" he cried, and sprinted off, back through the dusty house.

18

Pip and the Spirit Snatcher

Pip peered in through the bookshop window. Julius wasn't there, but neither was Mr Whipple. It seemed to be completely empty, although the lights were on and the sign on the door said *OPEN*. Pip stepped inside, peering around.

"Hello?" he called. "Is anyone there?"

There was no answer. Pip wandered past the bookshelves and up to the counter. The computer was turned on, and a mug of tea stood next to a glowing desk lamp. Pip put his hand to the side of the china mug – it was still warm. Mr Whipple must have just stepped out for a minute, or perhaps he had gone upstairs or into the storeroom. He immediately looked for the book on spirit snatchers but it had vanished.

"Hello?" he called again, more loudly this time. The

door into the back of the shop was locked, so Pip was unable to explore further. Instead he paced about the shop, still looking for the book while keeping an eye out for Julius. He was still clutching the torch.

Pip paused in front of the fireplace and gazed into the mirror above it. Its surface was so clouded that he couldn't even see a trace of his reflection. It was just like the mirror in his bedroom, which remained dull and opaque, no matter how much he tried to clean it. Pip leaned forwards and scrubbed at the mirror with his sleeve, then scratched at it with his fingernail, but it made no difference.

"What's that you're doing, Pip?"

Pip jumped in shock. He whirled around, then felt relief wash over him. It was just Mr Whipple, who was wrapped up in a shapeless brown coat, a parcel of books under his arm. He looked cold and windswept, and his nose was bright red. He seemed a little surprised to see Pip, and he set the books down upon the table in front of the window.

"I just popped out to retrieve a delivery," he said. "I should really have shut the shop, but I'm ashamed to say I forgot."

"I need to talk to you about Julius," said Pip urgently.

"He's the spirit snatcher."

"Pip," sighed Mr Whipple. "Do you really think that *Julius* is the spirit snatcher?"

"Yes!" cried Pip impatiently. "It all fits. I know he's your assistant, but you've got to believe me."

"You're on the wrong track again, Pip," said Mr Whipple with a sigh, as he closed the door of the bookshop. He turned the key in the lock, and put the key into his pocket. "Forgive me for saying this, but you'd make a terrible detective. I thought you'd figured it out when I saw you examining the mirror."

"What do you mean?" Pip was confused. "Look, let me explain," he continued. "Julius's—"

But Mr Whipple held up his hand, cutting him off.

"Julius is nothing more than a foolish student who was in dire need of draining. Or calming, as my dear friend Miss Qwirm would put it. We all have our preferred way of describing the process."

"It's...*you*?" Pip croaked. He gazed into Mr Whipple's round, cheerful face, although it wasn't looking quite so cheerful now. The bookseller's features were lit up with a curious expression – a mixture of pride and hunger – that Pip found deeply unsettling.

"Octavian Alfred Whipple, at your service," said Mr

Whipple. "But few people know me well enough to call me by my first name."

Pip shook his head.

"I don't understand…" he began. "You were *helping* us."

"It seemed like that, didn't it?" he replied. "Feeding you little snippets of information about protective charms, steering you in the wrong direction. It was the best way of distracting you both, until you turned thirteen and I had the opportunity to strike. It's been quite amusing to watch you run about, not thinking for a moment that it was me all along. There were so many better candidates – Julius, for instance. Or Sir Maxim – he made such a believable villain, didn't he? The only disappointment was that he refrained from killing you. I'd no idea he had such a strong moral code."

"But you can't be the spirit snatcher," said Pip. "You're a librus…Fliss said. You absorb books."

"It's simply a rumour I started years ago," replied Mr Whipple, with a small shake of his head. "I have an excellent memory, that's all."

Pip couldn't believe what he was hearing. He just stood there, staring at the old bookseller.

"You must understand that I can't let you out now,

Pip," said Mr Whipple, sounding almost apologetic. "You've had a remarkably lucky run of it. I meant to take your spirit on Halloween, as soon as you turned thirteen. But I hadn't planned on poor impulsive Fliss giving you her dog. I had to make do with her instead. It was quite sad really. She was so bright, so convinced that she would be safe. But as you saw, it doesn't matter who you are or how many people are looking out for you – spirit snatchers always get their victims in the end."

"How could you?" asked Pip. "Fliss thought you were her friend."

"I've been a spirit snatcher for over seven hundred years," replied Mr Whipple. "Do you realize how many people I've seen come and go in that time? After a while, you realize how fleeting it all is. You stop caring. Fliss doesn't matter. Your parents don't matter. You don't matter."

"What about Mr Bletchley?" asked Pip, still struggling to understand what had made Mr Whipple attack so many people. "He was older than a regular person, but you still went for him."

"He'd found out about me," said Mr Whipple. "He worked out that I wasn't a librus – he kept coming over to the shop and asking me endless questions about the history of food. Eventually, he realized that my memory had its limits. He assumed I was human, and trying to conceal it. Then, quite by accident, he spotted me transforming in the alleyway, just after I'd drained your parents, and of course, he realized what I really am. He promised to keep quiet, but I knew he'd let something slip. He was so very fond of talking. Draining him was the only thing to do."

"Why do you care so much about being found out?" asked Pip. "I mean, Sir Maxim's a vampire and he's not worrying about someone from Elbow Alley coming at him with a load of garlic, is he?"

"Because of what happened before," snapped Mr Whipple and he looked furious now. "There used to be thousands of spirit snatchers in England alone – we hunted where we pleased. We drained magical beings as well as humans – those with magic were better, as they usually had more spirit to feed on. Then, the magical community turned against us. They were furious at being drained, so they hunted us to the point of extinction, before they realized that they had a use for us after all, to stop humans from discovering them. A sort of truce was called – the surviving spirit snatchers agreed not to harm other magical beings, and so the present situation evolved. We each have our own area to hunt in, and we enable the magical communities to exist undetected. But we never forgot what they did to us, which is why we keep our identities hidden, to prevent anything of the kind happening again. And although few magical beings remember what happened with the spirit snatchers all those centuries ago, they are dimly aware that we could turn upon them once more, if we chose to."

"Why hasn't anyone else told me this?" said Pip. "I've been asking everyone, and no one's mentioned a battle between spirit snatchers and magical beings."

"It's fallen out of common memory now," replied Mr Whipple. "No other magical creature lasts nearly as long as we do, and I've made it my personal quest over the centuries to destroy any book that mentions it – being a bookseller puts me in an excellent position for that. That book you spotted yesterday was burned right after you left the shop."

He took a step closer to Pip, with a rather horrible expression on his face.

"Stop!" yelled Pip, and brandished his torch at Mr Whipple as if it was a sword. "Give everyone their spirits back or else I'm going to destroy you."

To his surprise, the bookseller started laughing.

"I'm not going to do that, Pip," he said, shaking his head. "And neither are you."

"Aren't I?" said Pip, furious now. He pressed the button and a bright blast of light erupted from the torch and hit Mr Whipple full in the face.

The bookseller simply blinked. Pip realized his mistake at once. Mr Whipple hadn't transformed yet. Pip kept the torch angled at Mr Whipple's face, determined to get him the moment he assumed his other form.

"Please stop this, Pip," said Mr Whipple, shielding his eyes and frowning. "It really is extremely annoying and you are completely misguided, as usual."

"What do you mean?" asked Pip suspiciously, lowering the torch a fraction.

"Spirit snatchers prefer to hunt at night but light won't destroy us. It would take more than a torch to kill me. There is only one thing that can stop me and it's something that you don't have."

Mr Whipple gave a tiny involuntary glance towards the clouded-over mirror and something clicked into place in Pip's brain. The fogged-up mirror in his bedroom; the strange curtains that hung next to the looking glasses in Miss Qwirm's drawing room; even the way that the mirrored bar in the Ragged Hare had been shattered into tiny fragments. A mirror would turn the spirit snatcher back upon itself, just like the book had said.

"It's mirrors!" he cried. "You can't look in mirrors, can you? That's your weak point!"

"Yes," said Mr Whipple, and to Pip's surprise he smiled at him, as if he was pleased that he had finally worked out the right answer. "Although we can use a mirror like anyone else when we're in our human form, it becomes dangerous when we've transformed. The sheer force and energy we emit to drain someone's spirit is incredibly powerful – if we accidentally turned our own power upon ourselves, it would destroy us. Fortunately, I've learned how to cloud over a mirror if I need to – you learn all sorts of useful things in books."

Pip was scanning the room, hoping to spot something else that was reflective. He wished fervently that he had his mobile phone with him, although he wasn't sure if a camera screen was the same thing as a mirror. Mr Whipple looked amused, as if he knew exactly what Pip was thinking.

"You won't find one," he said. "You're out of luck, Pip."

Abandoning any hope of finding a mirror, Pip went for the next best thing – a weapon. The torch wasn't going to be much use, so he dashed over to the fireplace and seized a long iron poker instead.

Mr Whipple laughed softly.

"That isn't going to be much good against me," he said, standing back out of reach of the poker. "Once I've transformed, no weapon or locked door can stop me. I can go anywhere and find anyone I please."

All Pip wanted was to get away. If he could just escape, he could find a mirror, retrieve Splodge and maybe even get some help.

"Being drained is not as bad as you might think," said Mr Whipple. "I believe it's not even painful. I have to do it, you see, now that you know too much. Why not just accept it? Your parents, Fliss, you'll be just like them. No more worrying. Everything will be simple, easy. Having too much spirit can be a terrible burden. Being drained is a much easier way of living – it takes the edge off, stops you caring so much."

"I don't want to live like that," said Pip, and he hurled the poker straight at the shop window. Pip held his breath as it flew through the air, waiting for the glass to shatter, readying himself to dive through and race to safety. But the poker bounced right off the window and fell to the floor with a clang.

"Shatterproof glass," said Mr Whipple calmly. "You can't be too careful nowadays."

He advanced on Pip, his figure becoming blurry at the edges as mist slowly seeped out of him.

"I'm going to enjoy this," said the bookseller, his voice echoing around the room as his features dissolved. "The longer the hunt, the more you savour the reward. I underestimated you, Pip. When I met you first, I thought you were remarkably weak-spirited. But there's more to you after all. Quite the feast. You know, spirit snatchers always show mercy on their victims – they never drain them entirely, they always leave them enough life to carry on. But perhaps, in your case, I might go a little further…"

His voice faded away entirely as the mist rose and swirled in a column, the same mist that Pip had seen before. There was the face, the blank voids of the eyes and nose and the gaping black mouth with long snapping teeth, wrought out of vapour but still terrifying. Pip remembered the banshee's song, less than an hour before, and Mapullan's words came back to him: "Somebody is about to die."

Pip backed away from the spirit snatcher's rising form, until he came to a halt against the hard edge of the desk. He stood as close to the light as he could, hoping that it might give him some protection, but the mist continued to advance upon him. Then he felt it, the same tugging feeling that he had experienced when the spirit snatcher had tried to drain him that first night in Elbow Alley. It was as if a tremendous force was ripping through his body and sucking his insides out. Pip's clenched fist brushed against something in his coat pocket, and he remembered it was the amulet. The useless amulet that wasn't really an amulet at all, just a cheap piece of mirrored metal.

The realization jolted through him, and he fought to keep his mind clear as he pulled out the amulet and held it up. The mist continued to swirl in front of him, stronger than ever, and the sound of laughter echoed around the room, cruel and amused. Pip caught sight of his own reflection in the back of the amulet, of his petrified, fear-ridden face. He felt oddly detached now, as if all of this was happening to someone else, as his spirit slowly leached from him into the mist that was about to swallow him up.

The spirit snatcher made a horrible hissing noise, so

loud and terrible that Pip jumped in shock. The amulet slipped from his fingers and rolled across the floor. He dropped to his hands and knees and crawled after it, even as the mist closed in around him, so he was feeling his way rather than being able to see. He crashed into the heavy oak counter, hardly feeling the pain, and then his searching fingers closed upon the amulet.

By now, the spirit snatcher seemed to have somehow seeped inside him, and Pip's brain felt so foggy and clouded that he was hardly able to think. But somehow, using every last bit of his effort, he held up the amulet, so that its mirrored surface gleamed in the lamplight, and shone directly into the mist.

There was an instant, awful screech. It was worse than the sound of fingernails scraping across a blackboard, more deafening than the sound of a siren, and more dreadful than the blackest of nightmares.

Pip clapped his hands over his ears, trying to drown it out, but then the column of mist exploded. Vapour shot outwards in all directions, fracturing into smaller and smaller bits, until all that was left was a light rain that softly fell upon Pip and the bookshop for a few moments before even that stopped.

Still reeling with the shock, Pip stared wildly around

the room. There was no trace of Mr Whipple. The keys to the shop – the ones that had been in the bookseller's pocket – were lying on the floor. The air felt different – it was warmer and somehow brighter, as if a heavy weight had been lifted. Pip stared at the key, as it slowly sunk in. He'd done it. The spirit snatcher was gone.

19

Afterwards

As Pip let himself out of the bookshop and stepped out into Elbow Alley, he felt like laughing with sheer relief. He was hardly able to believe what had just happened. There was a light on in The Ragged Hare, and as he drew near, Splodge bounded out of the pub, closely followed by Fliss.

"Pip!" she yelled, and launched herself at him, hugging him so tightly that he almost fell over.

"You're back!" he cried, as Splodge leaped around them, barking with joy.

"It was so weird," she said, as she let Pip go. "It was like being asleep – I hardly knew what was going on, then I came to about five minutes ago and remembered everything. What happened? Did you stop the spirit snatcher?"

"Yes," said Pip. "It was Mr Whipple."

"Mr Whipple?" cried Fliss, looking dumbfounded.

"I thought it was Julius, so I went over to find him, but Mr Whipple cornered me instead," said Pip. He told Fliss what had happened in the bookshop.

"That sneaky, two-faced *monster*!" she burst out as soon as Pip had finished. "After all that time, pretending to be my friend, he goes and spirit-snatches me the night of my birthday!"

"I shouldn't have taken Splodge," said Pip.

"I thought I'd be fine," muttered Fliss in a downcast voice. "I thought being half-werewolf would mean I wouldn't get attacked. But this proves it – I haven't inherited anything magical. I'm just a boring human."

"It doesn't mean anything," said Pip firmly. "They've always been able to attack magical beings as well as humans. It even got your dad."

"What?" cried Fliss, and fear flooded her face.

She whirled into the pub, dragging Pip with her.

"Dad?" she yelled. "Where are you?"

At that moment, Mr Wells returned, looking somewhat dishevelled and wearing an air of confusion, like someone who had just woken up from a very strange dream.

"Are you all right?" Fliss said urgently. "What's your favourite food? Can you sing me a tune?"

"Steak, very rare, and no I won't," replied Fliss's father, who was shaking his head in a very doglike fashion, as if he was trying to get water out of his ear. "Luckily the full moon's clouded over. Did that spirit snatcher get me? Something happened, didn't it?"

"Pip destroyed it," said Fliss proudly, and began to tell her father everything that had happened, as he started to clear up the mess behind the bar. However, she broke off mid-sentence as a slim woman with braided hair appeared in the doorway to the pub. Pip recognized her from the volcano photograph – it was Fliss's mother. She had an enormous canvas holdall slung over her shoulder and was staring at her daughter with an expression somewhere between shock and relief.

"Mum!" yelled Fliss, and ran straight into her mother's arms.

"I came back as soon as I heard," said Fliss's mother, hugging her tightly. "I thought you'd been spirit-snatched."

Fliss's father had joined them too and Pip hung back, not wanting to disturb the family reunion. For a moment, he felt a little bit lonely, and then he spotted something moving in the darkest corner of the pub. It had no features, it was just a silhouette of a man, the same colour as the walls. Yet Pip recognized who it was at once, and went towards it.

"You survived," whispered Mapullan. "I'm glad."

"Wait…" said Pip, but at that moment Penny burst in through the door, accompanied by Mr Bletchley, and the shapeshifter melted away.

"He's recovered!" cried Penny, gesturing at Mr Bletchley, her face lit up with joy. "Look at him!"

News travelled fast in Elbow Alley, and within minutes the pub was packed. Pip found that he was having to repeat the story of how he had stopped Mr Whipple over and over again as more of the other residents arrived. Most of them were celebrating, but there were a few who seemed troubled by the news, such as Sir Maxim, who had swept into the pub, looking very serious.

"If the spirit snatcher has gone, then Elbow Alley is unprotected," he said, frowning at Pip. "I don't blame you for what you've done – you were only trying to survive – but surely that leaves Elbow Alley open to discovery…"

"We'll be fine," said Mr Wells in his deep voice. "If

anyone threatens us, I'll tear them limb from limb."

Others were listening now.

"After all that's happened, I never want to encounter a spirit snatcher again," piped up Mr Bletchley.

"Neither do I," cried Penny. "There are plenty of other magical communities that have nothing to do with them. Why can't we be like those? When you think of all the trouble it caused…" Her eyes fell on Mr Wells.

"I daresay you'd have never gone after me, if you hadn't been spirit-snatched," she said.

"Of course he wouldn't!" said Fliss's mother, coming to her husband's defence at once. "He would never have been running loose, for one thing."

"You've all got powers of your own." Pip spoke up as he looked around the crowd. "You don't need a spirit snatcher to protect you."

His eyes locked with Sir Maxim's. There was a long pause, as the vampire seemed to consider everything that had been said.

"After all that has happened, perhaps it would be best for us to manage on our own," said Sir Maxim at last.

"There'll be no more spirit snatchers in Elbow Alley," Penny called. "And it's thanks to this young man. To Pip," she cried and raised her glass in the air. To Pip's surprise, everyone followed suit, echoing his name. As he looked around at the sea of familiar faces, he found himself beaming. He had never felt so proud.

Someone turned on the jukebox again and music flooded the pub. Pip took advantage of the uproar to slip away, because more than anything else, he wanted to see his parents. Surely their spirits had been returned to them, surely they were back to their old selves?

He didn't even have to go outside – he met them at the door.

"Pip!" cried Mrs Ruskin, pulling him into a hug. "We'd just come out to look for you – we were so worried!"

"I went upstairs to check on you and you'd gone," said his father, patting him on the shoulder. "I thought it was because of something we'd done – I haven't been feeling myself lately. We've been neglecting you, Pip."

"It's fine," said Pip, beaming at them. "It doesn't matter."

"It does matter," insisted Mrs Ruskin, who seemed reluctant to let him go. "I can't understand what your father and I have been doing for the last week, but the one thing I do know is that we haven't been there for you. I knew you didn't want to move here – I could tell you were unhappy."

"I like it here now," said Pip. "Honestly, I'm glad we moved."

It was true. There was nowhere he'd rather be.

Aisling came up behind them and smiled at Pip.

"I've just heard about what happened, Pip," she said. "I never know who it is I'm singing about – I'm very glad it wasn't you."

She disappeared into the pub. Pip's parents peered through the doorway, wide-eyed.

"Do you know those people, Pip?" asked his mother in surprise.

"I do," said Pip, grinning. "Why don't you come in and meet them?"

He led the way back into The Ragged Hare, and began to introduce his parents to everyone – to Fliss and her mother and father, to Seymour and Deathly, and to Sir Maxim and his collection of pale-faced gallery assistants. Before long, they all got swept up in the party, and Mrs Ruskin was chatting happily to Penny, while Mr Ruskin had become absorbed in a long and earnest discussion with Mr Bletchley about collecting antique food.

"I'd love to see your shop," Pip could hear his father spluttering, almost falling over his words in his eagerness. Mr Bletchley was as flushed as it was possible for a ghost to get, having finally found someone who was hanging on his every word. Pip went over to his father and said, in a low voice.

"Can I speak to you for a minute?"

Mr Ruskin nodded and turned to his son, while Mr Bletchley was instantly surrounded by the three Shuttleworth sisters from the hat shop. Mr Bletchley's run-in with the spirit snatcher had made him extremely popular.

"Did you notice anything about Mr Bletchley?" Pip asked his father.

"What?" said Mr Ruskin, looking perplexed. "He seems like a very nice man. Terribly interesting."

He bounced up and down on the soles of his feet as if he couldn't wait to get back to the conversation. But Pip hadn't finished. He was determined to see if his parents would spot what was going on.

"Look closely at him," said Pip. "You can see right through him."

Mr Ruskin stared hard at Mr Bletchley for a moment and frowned.

"What do you mean?" he said. "I don't understand."

"You don't notice anything strange about anyone in here?" Pip tried again. "Nothing at all?" He pointed at

Penny, whose claws were sticking out from the bottom of her coat as she perched on a bar stool. She was still talking to Mrs Ruskin, who didn't seem to have noticed the claws either.

Mr Ruskin frowned.

"They're all a bit eccentric, I suppose," he said finally. "But I am too. What's wrong with that?"

"Nothing," said Pip, feeling relieved but also very confused. Why couldn't his parents see what was right under their noses?

Mr Ruskin patted him on the shoulder again, still looking a little puzzled, then Mr Bletchley beckoned him over. Mr Ruskin looked longingly towards him.

"Do you mind if I…"

"Of course not," said Pip. "I'll see you later."

He watched as his father rushed off, trying to figure out how his parents could be so blind to their surroundings.

"They're adults," said Fliss, and Pip realized that she and Splodge had overheard the entire conversation. "They'll have got set in their ways by now. No matter how open-minded they are, if they've decided something doesn't exist, they won't be able to see it."

"You really think they'll be able to live in Elbow Alley without working out what's going on?" said Pip.

"Depends," said Fliss. "Do either of them believe in ghosts?"

Pip shook his head.

"Vampires? Ghouls? Banshees?"

"Nope," said Pip.

"Werewolves?" asked Fliss, with a grin.

"Definitely not."

"Then they won't see them for what they truly are," she said. "Anyway, my mum can keep an eye on them. She's learned how to live in the magical world as well as the human one."

Pip looked at his parents, chatting away happily, completely oblivious to the fact they were talking to a harpy, a ghost and a trio of elderly sylphs.

"I just want them to be safe," he said. "That's it." He realized that he meant every word. He no longer cared what they looked like, or how they behaved, or if his mother wanted to serve incredibly smelly fermented food at every single mealtime. None of it mattered, not really, as long as they were safe and happy.

"They will be," said Fliss. "After what you did, no one will lay a finger on them. You belong here now, so they do too."

She looked at Pip, a flicker of worry crossing her face.

"You *are* going to stay, aren't you?" she asked. Splodge was looking at Pip too, his ears pricked up expectantly.

"Yeah," said Pip and he grinned at them both. "I think we are."

A week later, Pip was helping his father to make the finishing touches to his shop. They had ripped the newspaper off the windows and cleaned the glass until it sparkled, chased away the spiders, painted the walls and swept the floors. All the bits and pieces that Mr Ruskin had collected over the years looked quite good now that there was enough space to see everything properly. Pip and Fliss had helped to arrange it all, and it finally resembled a proper shop. It had opened for the first time that morning, and already two customers had come in and bought things. Mr Ruskin was over the moon.

The flat upstairs looked different too – all the boxes had been unpacked, the pile of old computers had been disposed of, along with the disgusting old carpets. The whole place had been washed, scrubbed and polished until every surface shone. The atmosphere couldn't be more different. Mrs Ruskin rushed happily off to work each day, and Mr Ruskin hadn't turned the television on once.

Everything was full of life and laughter now that Pip's parents had regained their spirits. In fact, it was even better than before. Pip no longer felt the urge to curl up and die at the sight of his father's gold corduroy suit or his mother's habit of carrying jars of pickles in her handbag – he realized that it was simply part of who they were. In any case, compared to the other residents of Elbow Alley, his parents seemed almost normal.

"Wow," said Fliss, coming into the shop and looking around in amazement, while Splodge sniffed at the furniture, inspecting it all carefully. "This is fantastic."

"I know," said Pip proudly.

"I couldn't have done it without you two," said Mr Ruskin, who was sitting behind the brand-new counter, arranging a stack of equally brand-new business cards. "It's going to be a huge success, I can feel it."

"Can you spare Pip for a bit?" asked Fliss.

"Of course!" Mr Ruskin cried merrily. "Off you go – I've got everything under control."

"Julius is back," said Fliss, as soon as they were outside. "He's clearing out Mr Whipple's shop."

She pointed up the alley. Towers of boxes were stacked outside Mr Whipple's bookshop. Just then, Julius came out with another box and placed it on top of a teetering pile. It toppled over and books flew in all directions. Pip and Fliss hurried over to help, although they hadn't spoken to Julius since Mr Whipple had gone.

"Thank you," said Julius in an unusually friendly voice, as they crammed handfuls of books back into their containers.

"Are you closing the shop?" asked Pip.

"No," said Julius. "Just having a clear-out."

He was standing straighter and looked more alert than they had ever seen him. The sullen frown had disappeared off his face and he looked much younger. He was looking at Pip and Fliss curiously, as if he couldn't quite remember where he'd seen them before.

"Can't think where Whipple has got to," he said, more to himself than to them, as they went back inside the shop. "But if he's done a runner, then I'm free to do what I please. It's my shop, after all."

"I thought it was Mr Whipple's shop," said Fliss, confused. "It was his name above the door. Whipple & Co."

"It's mine," repeated Julius, with a wry smile. "I let Whipple set up here, about a decade ago, and ended up working for him. I don't know why I agreed to it – I must have been mad. Still, I'm going to make up for lost time.

I'm going to really put my mark on the business, run the place myself."

He got out a feather duster and began dusting down the shelves of leather-bound volumes, whistling to himself under his breath.

"He's a lot nicer now that he's got his spirit back," said Fliss quietly, and Pip nodded in agreement.

He looked around the shop, remembering everything that had happened there. His eyes fell upon the mirror above the fireplace and, to his surprise, he saw his reflection looking back at him.

"Look," he said to Fliss. "It must have cleared after Mr Whipple vanished – it was clouded over before. I didn't think to check it at the time."

"Why would you?" said Fliss. "I mean, you had bigger things to worry about than the state of an old mirror."

"The one in my bedroom's gone back to normal, too," said Pip thoughtfully.

"Well, that's useful," said Fliss, whose mind seemed to be on other things. She whistled at Splodge, who had been making a thorough investigation of the bookshop's dustbin. The bin toppled over with a loud clang as Splodge clambered out, covered in dust and clutching the remains of an ancient sandwich between his jaws.

Pip and Fliss said goodbye to Julius, who waved at them cheerily from halfway up the library ladder. The change in him was really quite remarkable and Pip felt another surge of happiness that everyone in Elbow Alley was finally free from the spirit snatcher.

"Anyway, I wanted to ask you, are you still starting at that new school next week?" asked Fliss, as they left the shop. "The one round the corner from St Sepulchre's?"

"Yeah," said Pip. The only downside to his parents' full recovery was that they had become very aware that he still hadn't started at a London school. "It looks okay, I guess."

He couldn't really drum up much enthusiasm for it, even though it sounded much better than the school he'd attended in Norwich.

"Well I've got some news for you," announced Fliss triumphantly. "I've decided I'm going to be a magical researcher like my mother. She's been telling me all about her trip to that haunted island – it sounds really dangerous, even better than being a werewolf. But if I want to do that, I'll have to go to regular school and learn about history and geography before I can specialize in the supernatural stuff. We'll be in the same class!"

Pip couldn't believe it. Having Fliss there, having a

real friend, would change everything. He'd have someone to sit next to, someone who already knew and didn't care about his weird lunches, and most importantly, someone who was on his side.

"What's the matter?" asked Fliss. "Aren't you pleased? You'd better not ditch me once you start. You know, when you find some more *normal* friends."

She made a face, but Pip could tell that she was worried.

"Normal is boring," said Pip firmly. "I've had enough of trying to fit in. Life's much more fun when you decide to stand out."

"Well if you carry on wearing that jumper, you'll have no problem doing that," said Fliss, nodding at Pip's bright red jumper, the one with the fox on it. She was grinning now, looking as relieved as Pip felt. "I never thought I'd say this, but it's even better than my gold jumpsuit."

"It is, isn't it?" agreed Pip proudly. "And after everything we've been through, I think school's going to be a breeze."

They stayed outside the bookshop for a little while, leafing through the boxes of books. Across the road, Mr Bletchley was tenderly dusting the giant mouldy cheese in his shop window, and a few doors down, Annabelle and Sybil were rearranging their display of hats. Pip spotted a rat peering out from the mouth of a drainpipe outside the abandoned house, and guessed that it was Mapullan, still preferring to keep to the shadows. A rare blaze of November sunlight was shining down, and Pip looked up into the clear blue sky. He felt that anything was possible. And the best part about living in Elbow Alley was that you never knew what might happen next.

The End

Discover more pockets of magic that hide just out of sight, with another adventure from the imagination of Cat Gray...

"A non-stop adventure, full of spellbinding, sorcerers and selkies. Cat Gray's storytelling proves that magic really does exist."

Helena Duggan, author of *A Place Called Perfect*

ʽWelcome to ʾYowling – a secretive seaside village where magic is just one step away...

Max has spent years thinking he is cursed, because whenever he touches anything electrical it explodes. But then he is sent to Yowling and discovers he is a spellstopper, someone with the rare ability to drain dangerous build-ups of magic and fix misbehaving enchanted items.

When Max's grandfather is kidnapped by the cruel Keeper of the malfunctioning magical castle that floats in the bay, only Max's gift can save him. Together with his new friend Kit, Max throws himself into an adventure filled with villainous owls, psychic ice cream and man-eating goldfish. But can he really pull off the biggest spellstop ever?

**"A charming page-turner...
I lapped up every moment of this magical tale."**

Clare Povey, author of
The Unexpected Tale of Bastien Bon Livre

Acknowledgements

It's been almost four years since the first glimmers of this book came into my head on a damp and misty October morning in London. Since then, I published my debut novel *Spellstoppers*, and *The Spirit Snatcher* has been on quite the journey, one that's had all sorts of twists and turns to it. Like all big journeys, you rarely complete them alone, and I was fortunate to encounter plenty of help and encouragement along the way from my brilliant friends and family, with a few very special mentions owed to those who have had the most involvement in shaping *The Spirit Snatcher*.

The team at Usborne have done a terrific job in helping to bring this book into the world and I've been truly lucky to have worked with such a fantastic publisher. A huge thanks in particular to my editors Sarah Stewart and Rebecca Hill, for being so enthusiastic about the world of Elbow Alley and helping to hone the manuscript into its current form.

A big thank you to my agent, Silvia Molteni, for her tenacity and belief in this book from the start – I'm extremely grateful.

My sister, Becky Cole, has been unflaggingly encouraging throughout the entire process, even finding some wonderful young readers to provide early feedback on the manuscript. I'm very lucky to have her. My parents, too, have been incredibly supportive of my writing – I'm sure I'd have never become an author if it wasn't for their influence.

Finally, my husband, Tim, who has been subjected to the minute-by-minute progress of this book for nearly four years now, and is still as patient as ever. The residents of Elbow Alley thank you, as do I.

Cat Gray is an author and journalist. She started her journalism career while still a student, interviewing musicians and celebrities in between studying English Literature at Trinity College Dublin and the University of Cambridge. She then went on to work on magazines including *GQ* and *Harper's Bazaar*.

She's always believed that there's an adventure just around the corner, and this is reflected in her magical fantasy stories.

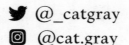 @_catgray
@cat.gray